PUFFIN

SPY PUPS

TRAINING SCHOOL

Andrew Cope lives in the middle of England. He is a footy fan and an avid reader. He hardly ever watches the telly. His favourite colour is orange and his favourite word is 'avid'. A few years ago Andrew's family adopted a dog from the RSPCA. To be honest, on the intelligence scale, she's pretty much at the bottom. And when looks were dished out she was at the back of the queue. She's got ridiculous ears and the most horrific dog breath. All in all, Lara hasn't got much going for her.

So why is it that Lara gets all the fuss and attention? At Spy Dog events, why do five hundred kids swarm around the dog, patting and stroking and rubbing her tummy, while Andrew twiddles his thumbs? Why do children squeal with excitement when Lara enters the room, but merely say, 'Oh, it's you,' when Andrew does?

I guess it's because Lara is the world's first ever Spy Dog. She goes on undercover missions and saves the world. And Andrew Cope is just an author.

If you want Lara or her puppy to visit your school, please email her at lara@artofbrilliance.co.uk. They'll probably have to bring Andrew Cope along too, but don't let that put you off. Or you can find out more about the Spy Dog and Spy Pups books online at *www.spydog451.co.uk*, where there are pictures, videos and competitions too!

SPY PUPS

TRAINING SCHOOL

ANDREW COPE

Illustrated by James de la Rue

PUFFIN

PUFFIN BOOKS

Published by the Penguin Group
Penguin Books Ltd, 80 Strand, London WC2R ORL, England
Penguin Group (USA) Inc., 375 Hudson Street, New York, New York 10014, USA
Penguin Group (Canada), 90 Eglinton Avenue East, Suite 700, Toronto, Ontario, Canada M4P 2Y3
(a division of Pearson Penguin Canada Inc.)
Penguin Ireland, 25 St Stephen's Green, Dublin 2, Ireland
(a division of Penguin Books Ltd)
Penguin Group (Australia), 250 Camberwell Road, Camberwell, Victoria 3124, Australia
(a division of Pearson Australia Group Pty Ltd)
Penguin Books India Pvt Ltd, 11 Community Centre, Panchsheel Park, New Delhi – 110 017, India
Penguin Group (NZ), 67 Apollo Drive, Rosedale, North Shore 0632, New Zealand
(a division of Pearson New Zealand Ltd)
Penguin Books (South Africa) (Pty) Ltd, Block D, Rosebank Office Park,
181 Jan Smuts Avenue, Parktown North, Gauteng 2193, South Africa

Penguin Books Ltd, Registered Offices: 80 Strand, London WC2R ORL, England

puffinbooks.com

First published 2012
001 – 10 9 8 7 6 5 4 3 2 1

Text copyright © Andrew Cope and Ann Coburn, 2012
Illustrations copyright © James de la Rue, 2012
All rights reserved

The moral right of the authors and illustrator has been asserted

Set in Bembo
Typeset by Palimpsest Book Production Limited, Falkirk, Stirlingshire
Printed in Great Britain by Clays Ltd, St Ives plc

British Library Cataloguing in Publication Data
A CIP catalogue record for this book is available from the British Library

ISBN: 978–0–141–33881–1

www.greenpenguin.co.uk

ALWAYS LEARNING   **PEARSON**

Contents

Contents

1. The Mask with Two Faces

'Follow me, folks!' the museum guide called. 'You're about to see one of the most important pieces of art in the whole world – and we're proud to have it on display in our very own Metropolitan Museum of Art, right here in New York!'

A crowd of tourists and a teacher with a party of schoolchildren followed the guide through a narrow tunnel into a round, windowless room. A circle in the middle of the room was roped off, leaving a strip of open floor around the edge. As the crowd shuffled in and lined up behind the rope barrier, two men in dark suits slipped into the room and stood behind the crowd, one on either side of the tunnel.

If anyone had looked at the pair, they would

have had a shock. The two men were identical in every detail, except that one had a mole on his right cheek and the other had exactly the same mole on his left cheek. Nobody did look, though; they were all too busy peering at the shadowy object roped off in the middle of the room.

'Here we go,' said the guide. 'Feast your eyes on the Janus mask!' He flicked a switch and a powerful spotlight snapped on.

The crowd gasped. The mask in the centre of the room was made of pure beaten gold; it gleamed softly as it turned on its pedestal. It

had two identical faces, one at the front and one at the back.

'Can I try it on?' asked a small girl.

'Sorry, sweetie,' said the guide. 'This isn't a fancy dress mask. It's priceless! It dates back to early Roman times and it's the only one of its kind.'

A boy raised his hand. 'Why does it have two faces?'

'Good question, son,' said the guide. 'Janus was a Roman god who could see both forward into the future and backward into the past, so the mask-maker gave him two faces. You could say Janus had eyes in the back of his head, just like your teacher here!'

The schoolchildren giggled.

'Yes, I do,' agreed the teacher. 'That's how I know some of you are eating candy right now, even though I told you no food in the museum!'

The children stopped giggling and there was a rustling as sweets were reluctantly pushed back into pockets. The adults in the crowd chuckled and then everyone turned back to studying the golden mask.

Everyone except the two dark-suited men. They were busy checking out the museum security instead. Their cold blue eyes took in the lasers, the security cameras and the pressure pad under the mask. Finally, they both focused on a thin steel ring set into the floor around the pedestal. They frowned. The steel ring was something new. What was it for? What did it do? Their eyes met and they both gave the slightest of shrugs.

Just then a boy in front of the men eased a bag of jelly babies back out of his pocket. The pair shared a smile and then bent down, one on each side of the boy.

'Teacher said no candy, kid!' hissed one of the men.

The boy jumped and, at the same time, the other man nudged his arm. A jelly baby flew from the bag, sailed over the rope barrier and bounced on to the floor beside the steel ring. The two men watched with interest to see what would happen next.

The jelly baby was instantly sliced in half as a cylinder shot up out of the steel ring. The cylinder zoomed upwards with a metallic hiss and locked into a groove in the roof, sealing the Janus mask behind a pillar of steel.

In the moment of stunned silence that

followed, one of the dark-suited men plucked the remaining jelly babies from the boy's hand. The boy began to cry.

'Simon!' roared the teacher. 'Was that your jelly baby?'

'It wasn't my fault! It was those nasty men!'

Simon turned and pointed behind him, but there was nobody there. The men had slipped away.

'Jelly baby, Brad?'

'Thanks, Chad. Don't mind if I do.'

Brad and Chad Onkers strolled away from the museum into Central Park, chewing on Simon's jelly babies. They found a quiet bench and sat down side by side.

'We must,' began Brad.

'Have that mask,' finished Chad.

'It's us!' began Brad.

'In gold!' finished Chad.

The Onkers twins turned on the bench so that they were back to back, and posed as the Janus mask. It was a spooky sight. Their spiky blond hair was exactly the same length and thickness, their noses had identical bumps across the bridge, and their chins both had a cleft down the middle which made them look like tiny bums. The only way to tell them apart was their moles.

'So. It's agreed. We steal,' began Chad.

'The Janus mask,' finished Brad.

'In time for,' began Chad.

'Our birthday next week,' finished Brad.

'Better than any cake!' they said together.

'But how,' asked Brad.

'Do we do it?' finished Chad.

'It'll be our toughest job yet,' said Brad.

'Let's think on it,' said Chad.

They sat on the bench until they had finished Simon's jelly babies, then they both shook their heads and stood up.

'Nothing yet,' said Chad.

'Me neither,' admitted Brad. 'We'll figure it out. We always do. Meanwhile, I gotta get to work.' He pulled an FBI badge from his pocket and hung it round his neck. The badge had his photograph on one side, and the words SPECIAL AGENT B. ONKERS on the other.

'I gotta get to work too,' said Chad, pulling a set of skeleton keys from his pocket and running them through his fingers.

'What's the heist this time?' asked Brad.

'Those two Picasso paintings in the mansion you were protecting a few months back.'

Brad's blue eyes gleamed greedily. 'They'll look lovely hanging on our wall. You got the codes for the burglar alarm?'

Chad nodded and tapped the side of his head. 'It's all in here. The layout of the mansion — everything. That night I spent there posing as you was very useful. You know, Brad, every art thief should have a twin working in the FBI!'

'And every FBI agent should have a twin working as an art thief!

'Two heads are better than one,' said Chad.

'Or two faces,' said Brad.

The Onkers twins leant their identical faces together and gave an identical evil laugh.

2. Riders on the Storm

The plane had nearly reached New York when the pilot sat forward with a frown. Flying conditions had been good all the way across the Atlantic, but now a bank of black cloud was boiling up on the horizon. The pilot checked the flight path. The plane was heading straight for the black clouds.

Hmm. They weren't in the forecast, she thought. *Maybe they're harmless.* Just then lightning began to flicker inside the clouds. *Or maybe not! It's a freak storm! Time to climb.*

The pilot checked the radar screens. There was no air traffic above her, so she put the plane into a steep climb, taking it high above the storm.

That's better. At least we'll be flying over it now. But we're still in for a bumpy ride. Time to wake my co-pilot.

She leant across and prodded the man snoring beside her.

'Sooo many baa-lambs . . .' mumbled Professor Cortex, opening his eyes. He blinked at the black and white dog sitting next to him in the cockpit. 'Oh hello, GM451.'

Lara couldn't help a doggy grin. Her old friend was one of the world's top scientists and the head of the British government's animal spying programme. He had a brain as big as a planet, yet here he was, baby-talking in his sleep. She raised an eyebrow at him. *Baa-lambs . . .?*

Professor Cortex blushed and straightened his bow tie. 'Ahem. I was dreaming about sheep. Must be all those fluffy white clouds out there.'

They're not white any more, Prof. Lara pointed a paw at the storm clouds. *And they're definitely not fluffy!*

'Have we reached New York?' Professor Cortex peered through the cockpit window and gave a high-pitched yelp when he saw the stormy sky. 'Good grief! Why didn't you wake me?'

Lara sighed. *I just did!*

'Looks like we're in for a rough ride, GM451,' said Professor Cortex. 'Do you think you can fly us through it?'

Lara looked at the specially adapted canine cockpit. She gave a determined nod, her sticky-up ear springing to attention. *Course I can, Prof! After all, I am the only black and white mutt ever to have gained her pilot's licence.*

Lara's chest swelled with pride as she remembered the day her instructor told her she had qualified as a pilot. *He told me I'd passed with 'flying colours'*, she smiled. *Nice line!* Back then, she had still been in active service as the world's first ever Spy Dog, trained by Professor Cortex. 'Lara' stood for Licenced Assault and Rescue Animal, and her code name had been GM451. Then, one dark day, Lara had nearly died on a mission.

She shuddered and touched a paw to her sticky-up ear, which had a bullet hole clean through it as a souvenir of her encounter with the arch-criminal Mr Big. After that, Professor Cortex had decided to retire her from active duty. Now Lara lived with the Cooks, her adopted family. Her pups, Star and Spud, were the professor's newest Spy Dogs, but she still liked to keep her skills up to scratch and she had been glad of the chance to fly again.

'That's the spirit, Lara!' said Professor Cortex, adjusting his headphones. 'You fly the plane and I'll talk to air traffic control; between us, we'll bring this plane in to land. But first I'd better warn our passengers.'

As Professor Cortex pressed the intercom button, Lara tightened her seat belt. Everyone she loved most in the world was on this plane. As well as her old friend Professor Cortex and his personal bodyguards Agents K and T, her pups Spud and Star were on-board, along with Mr and Mrs Cook and their children Ben, Sophie and Ollie. *I'm landing this plane safely,* she vowed. *And nothing, not even a freak storm, is going to stop me!*

No one in the passenger cabin had any idea of the drama unfolding in the cockpit. The British government plane had sixteen comfortable seats, arranged round four tables. Spud, Star, Ben and Sophie were sitting together at one table. Spud was munching his way through his third packet of crisps, Star was on her laptop checking out the FBI's 'most wanted' gallery, and Ben and Sophie were looking through a New York guidebook.

'I can't wait to ride in a yellow cab,' said Sophie.

'And I can't wait to climb up the Statue of Liberty,' said Ben.

'Like King Kong?' asked Ollie, from the table across the aisle.

Ben laughed. 'No, Ollie. I think I'll use the steps *inside* the building. Much safer.'

'Oh.' Ollie lost interest and went back to tormenting Agents K and T, who were sharing his table.

'Look at them, Spud, they're so excited!' yapped Star, nodding at Ben and Sophie. 'It was really nice of the prof to bring them along with us to New York.'

'S'pose so,' Spud muttered.

Star giggled. 'You're not still angry with the prof about those injections, are you? You know he had to vaccinate us so we could get our pet passports.'

Spud squirmed in his seat. 'Yes, but he didn't have to treat my bum like a dartboard! And how come we had to have rabies jabs, but the humans didn't? I mean, we all live in the same house in the same little English village. Rabies is when you go insane and start foaming at the mouth. The closest we get to that is when Ollie puts too much toothpaste on his brush.'

'That's what's so exciting,' yapped Star.

'What? Rabies?'

'No! It's exciting to be leaving our little village to work with the FBI in New York! It's what's been missing from our training so far, bro. After this, we'll be ready for Big City spying anywhere in the world! Admit it, Spud, you must be excited about getting out on the streets of one of the most exciting cities in the world. They call it the Big Apple!'

'Yeah, I am! And "big apple" reminds me. Isn't New York famous for its food? Huge portions too! Bagel stalls, burger stalls, donut stands, pancakes. I can't wait!' slurped Spud.

'Forget the food,' said Star, turning the screen of her laptop towards her brother. 'Look at these FBI "most wanted" mugshots. We'll be training with real heroes, Spud. FBI agents deal with armed baddies like this lot every day.'

'Well, we're no strangers to armed baddies either,' yawned Spud. 'Me and Ma have both been shot by one.' He tapped his bullet-holed left ear and discovered a drinking straw that he had stuck there for safe-keeping. 'Oh, that's where it went.' Spud yanked the straw out of the bullet hole, dropped it into his glass and slurped up some lemonade.

Star shook her head fondly at her brother. In many ways they were very different. Spud loved his food and had a plump belly to show for it; she loved to exercise and had lost all her puppy fat. Spud had black fur and floppy ears while she was black and white with one sticky-up ear, just like their mum. But she and Spud had two big things in common: they both loved adventure and they were both proud to be Spy Dogs! 'You're not fooling me, Spud. You can act as cool as you like; I know you're as excited as I am about this training.'

Spud gave a doggy grin. 'You got me, sis! I admit it. I'm so excited I might even forgive the prof for sticking needles in my bum.'

Across the aisle, Ollie had made a paper plane

out of his passenger sick bag. '*Nneeooowww!*' he yelled, zooming it past Agent K's head.

Agent K jumped. He was sweating and staring through the window at the plane wing as though it might drop off at any second.

'I don't get it,' Ollie declared. 'You're meant to be a big, tough personal bodyguard! Your job is really dangerous, with guns and walkie-talkies and fighting baddies and stuff. So how come you're scared of flying?'

Agent K didn't answer, so Ollie crashed his paper plane into the table with an ear-splitting '*Kaboom!*'. His hands leapt into the air in a mock explosion. 'Everyone dies!' Agent K gave a strangled squeak.

'Ollie! Leave Agent K alone!' ordered Mr Cook from the next table. 'Can't you see he's feeling a bit unwell?'

'Really, Agent K, there's no need to worry,' soothed Mrs Cook. 'Air travel is very safe – and it's been a smooth flight so far.'

'Very smooth,' beamed Mr Cook, waving an empty sick bag triumphantly. 'I haven't thrown up once, and you know what I'm like!'

Just then the plane lurched violently. Spud's glass bounced across the table, spraying him

with lemonade from nose to tail. Star avoided
the lemonade, but only because she had been
bounced from her seat into the aisle. Agent K
screamed when an oxygen mask fell on to his
head.

'What's happening?' yapped Star as she
scrambled back into her seat.

The cabin speakers clicked on. 'Ahem, sorry
about that little surprise,' said Professor Cortex,
the speakers making it sound like he was
holding his nose. 'I was just about to warn you,
but the storm beat me to it.'

'Storm!' squeaked Agent K.

17

'We're flying into a big one,' continued Professor Cortex. 'So you'd better put your seat belts on. Turbulence ahead.'

The speakers clicked off and everyone reached for their seat belts, except for Agent K, who had never taken his off. He reached for Ollie's seat belt instead and began to fasten it for him with shaking hands.

'What are turbulents?' asked the little boy. 'They sound cool. Are they monsters?'

'No. "Turbulence" is just a big word for a lot of wind,' said Sophie.

'Like Dad in the bathroom?'

'No, silly. Like a hurricane that throws you around a bit,' explained his sister.

'Sounds exciting,' beamed Ollie.

'Yes, it'll be fun! Like a roller coaster!' said Mrs Cook as brightly as she could.

There was another dramatic lurch and Mr Cook groaned and reached for his sick bag.

'I love roller coasters!' said Ollie, settling back to enjoy the ride. But as the plane began to buck across the sky like an overexcited kangaroo, nobody else looked as though they were having much fun at all.

3. A Very Close Shave

'K9TAX1 to Control Tower,' radioed Professor Cortex. 'Are we clear to land? Conditions are getting a bit bumpy up here. Over'

'K9TAX1, you're clear to land,' replied the Control Tower. 'But this storm is too big for you to fly around. The weather people are telling us that this is the worst lightning storm to hit the area in living memory. You'll have to descend through the cloud bank and use your flight deck instruments to navigate. We wish you well, K9TAX1,' crackled the voice. 'Remember, you'll have to go under. Over.'

'Roger that, Control Tower,' said Professor Cortex. 'Can't go over. Will go under. Over,' he repeated, casting a slightly confused glance at his canine co-pilot. He flicked a switch and

19

spoke to the cabin. 'We'll be landing very soon, folks, but we have to go through the storm, so stay belted up.' He switched off the intercom and looked at Lara. 'Ready, GM451?'

Lara cast a worried glance at the black clouds swirling below the plane and then checked all her instruments. *Hold on to your hat, Prof,* she nodded. *I'm going in!*

As soon as the plane flew down into the storm, black clouds blanketed the windscreen. The cockpit was plunged into darkness, apart from the bright green glow of the navigation screens. Suddenly, Lara was flying blind.

Yikes! Mustn't panic! I don't need to see where I'm going; the navigation screens have all the information I need. At least I hope so . . .

'Oof! Oww!' cried Professor Cortex as the plane began to jolt violently, jerking them around in their seats. Lara could hear similar barks and cries coming from the cabin behind her.

Hang on, pups! Hang on, everyone! We're halfway down . . .

Lara's heart was thumping. She focused on her instruments, checking the speed of her descent and adjusting her flight path. Rain lashed against the small aeroplane windscreen and it became eerily dark outside.

Two-thirds of the way down . . .

We're nearly there –

Suddenly, the cockpit was filled with a blinding white light. There was a loud bang, the plane shuddered and the navigation screens went dark. The cockpit crackled with electricity, making Lara's fur stand on end from her nose to her tail.

'Oh no!' gasped Professor Cortex. 'We've been struck by lightning!'

Tell me something I don't know, thought Lara, checking her controls.

'And all our screens are down!' the professor

added, running his hands through his hair, which was already standing out around his head like an electrically charged dandelion.

I said, tell me something I don't kn– oh, never mind. At least the engines haven't stopped working. That means I can still fly this thing. But which way?

Lara thought hard, considering her options. Her fuel was too low to head back above the clouds and wait for the storm to end. She couldn't fly out to the edge of the storm either; air traffic control had said the cloud bank was too wide. No, the only option was to keep going down until they came out underneath the storm clouds. *Hopefully, visibility will improve down there*, she thought.

'Prof?' she barked questioningly, pointing downwards.

Professor Cortex nodded. 'I agree, Lara. It's our only chance.'

Lara put the plane into a steep dive, cutting through the clouds. Lightning flashed all around her. The instruments on the panel were all dead. *I've got no idea about height or speed!* She began to sweat at the thought of the ground rushing up to meet them, but she kept her nerve and, finally, the plane broke through the base of the clouds and out into the rainy sky.

'Well done!' cried Professor Cortex as Lara pulled up the nose of the plane and levelled it out. 'Superb flying! But then I would expect nothing less of a trained Spy Dog.'

Hold your horses, Prof, we're not down yet, thought Lara. She scanned the ground, looking for the runway, but there was no tarmac below her, and no lights. Instead she was looking at a wide stretch of deep water. *Oops! I overshot. That's the Hudson River below.*

Lara looked up again and gave a yelp of shock. A huge, dark figure was looming out of the rain, right in front of the plane!

'Thank goodness for that,' yapped Star as the plane levelled out and the cabin stopped shuddering.

'Well, we're out of the storm,' said Ben, peering through the rain-splattered window. 'But we're nowhere near the airport; there's a river down there.'

'Good. That means I've got time for one more snack before we land,' woofed Spud, opening another packet of crisps.

Across the aisle, Mr Cook groaned at the

23

strong smell of cheese and onion and reached for another sick bag. He had already filled two.

'That was better than any roller coaster!' cried Ollie, bouncing in his seat. 'Let's do it again!'

Beside him, Agent K made a squawking sound. Ollie looked across and saw tears rolling down the agent's terrified face. 'Aww, it's all right, Agent K. Don't be scared. We won't do it again if you don't want to,' he soothed, patting the crying bodyguard on the arm.

'*Waahhh!*' wailed Agent K.

Agent T folded his arms and looked embarrassed, but Ollie reached into his rucksack and pulled out his teddy bear. 'I think you need this more than me,' he said, handing it to Agent K.

On the next table, Mr Cook folded over the top of his third sick bag and gave a shaky sigh.

'Are you all right, dear?' asked Mrs Cook. 'You still look a bit green.'

A bit? thought Star, studying Mr Cook's face. *Kermit the frog's got nothing on him!*

'I'll be fine now, as long as there are no more sudden movements.'

Without warning, the plane tipped over on

to its side and swerved hard to the left. The engines roared and everything slid off the tables. Mr Cook, Agent K and Agent T were squashed up against their side of the plane, which had suddenly become the floor, and Mrs Cook and Ollie were pressed on top of them. Ben, Sophie, Spud and Star were left hanging in their seat belts, with a clear view through the window below.

They saw a huge eye, looking in at them.

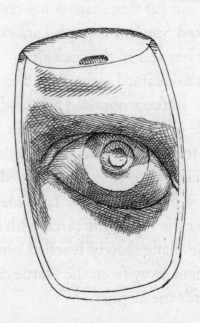

4. Welcome to New York

'It's a turbulent!' cried Ollie.

'It's the Statue of Liberty!' yelled Sophie at the same time, wincing as the plane just missed one of the spikes around Liberty's head.

'Watch out for that massive ice-cream cone, Ma!' barked Spud as though Lara could hear him from her seat in the cockpit.

Everyone screamed as the plane boomeranged round the statue's upraised arm and climbed up the side of the flaming torch that Spud had mistaken for an ice-cream cone.

'We're not going to make it!' cried Ben.

But they did. Somehow, Lara managed to scrape over the top of the torch with metres to spare. The plane slowly levelled out and she piloted them away from the Statue of Liberty and towards the airport.

It was Sophie who finally broke the shocked silence in the cabin. 'Well, Ben,' she said faintly. 'You said you wanted to see the Statue of Liberty.'

'Yes, but not that close up!' said Ben.

Minutes later, the runway lights appeared below them.

Lara stayed cool in the cockpit. The man on the other end of the radio talked her in. *Lower*, she thought. *Ease off the power. Undercarriage down. And a little lower still . . .*

The wheels screeched on the tarmac and Professor Cortex punched the air in delight. The thrust of the engines slowed the aircraft. 'You've done it, GM451,' he shouted. He flicked the switch and announced to the passengers, 'GM451 has successfully completed her first emergency landing . . . in the worst storm for fifty years . . . and she gave us a close-up view of some of the sights along the way!'

The plane taxied in to cheering and applause from the passengers. Agent K squeezed the teddy bear, secretly hoping Ollie would let him hold on to it for a little bit longer.

The plane was directed to a private hangar

where a sleek, black stretch limo was waiting for them. As the plane taxied to a halt and the airport ground staff brought a set of steps up to the door, a black-suited FBI agent clambered from the limo and stood, arms folded.

'Ready, everyone?' cried Professor Cortex, bursting through the dividing door between the cabin and the cockpit, with Lara at his heels. Everyone stared at them in surprise. Professor Cortex's bow tie had escaped from his collar and was wrapped round his dandelion hair like an Alice band, and Lara's fur was standing on end.

'Ma! You look like a toilet brush!' yapped Spud.

'Was it the shock?' asked Star.

'No. There was a lot of static electricity in the cockpit.' Lara shook herself, which only made her fur stick out more, and then looked around at the passengers in the cabin. Spud was covered in cheese and onion crisps, which were glued to the sticky lemonade in his fur. Mr Cook had his head buried in yet another sick bag, and Agent K was clutching a teddy bear and sucking his thumb. 'You lot don't look much better,' she woofed. 'Perhaps we should

take a minute to sort ourselves out before we leave the plane.'

But Professor Cortex was already opening the door. 'Let's go!' he ordered. 'Time to meet our hosts.'

'Just a minute,' began Agent T, pointing at the professor's hairdo.

'I don't have a minute, Agent T!' interrupted Professor Cortex. 'Thanks to Lara, we made it through the storm, but we mustn't keep the FBI waiting any longer.'

'Hold on, Professor,' said Sophie, pulling a hairbrush from her bag. 'Let me just –'

'No time for grooming, Sophie,' said Professor Cortex sternly. 'I have important government business to attend to. Chop-chop!'

Professor Cortex stepped from the plane and set off down the steps. Lara shrugged at Sophie and then followed the professor out.

The FBI agent strode from the car to meet them at the bottom of the steps. 'Professor Cortex?' he said, giving the professor's crazy hairdo a disbelieving stare.

'At your service,' said Professor Cortex.

'I'm Special Agent Brad Onkers,' growled the FBI man.

'Pleased to meet you, Agent Onkers,' said Professor Cortex. 'Let me introduce the world's finest secret agent, GM451.'

Brad curled his lip as he looked down at Lara. He considered himself to be the world's top agent. '*This* mutt is one of your famous Spy Dogs?'

Lara curled her own lip and gave Agent Onkers one of her meanest stares in return. *You'd better believe it, buddy!*

'That's right,' said Professor Cortex proudly. 'And here come the other two,' he added as Star and Spud bounded down the steps to join them.

'But – they're just a pair of mucky pups,' said Onkers, sneering at the trail of crisp crumbs Spud had left.

You're no oil painting yourself, thought Spud. *You've got a bum-chin!*

'Who does he think *he* is?' yapped Star.

Spud peered up at the FBI agent's identity tag. 'Special Agent B. Onkers,' he read. 'Bonkers! Ha! Good name for him!'

'Don't let appearances fool you, Agent Onkers,' said Professor Cortex as Spud and Star leant together, sniggering. 'These pups are highly trained agents.'

'Yeah, right,' said Brad. 'Next you'll be telling me that those two over there are highly trained bodyguards.'

They all looked round. Agent K was staggering down the steps from the plane, supported by Agent T. He was still clutching Ollie's teddy bear.

'They are!' Professor Cortex protested. 'Agent K! Take your thumb out of your mouth!'

Brad raised an eyebrow. 'Pardon me for saying so, sir, but those two look about as

tough as a pair of baby bun-
nies.'

'Watch it, Onkers!'
growled Spud, sizing up
the FBI agent's leg.

'Spud!' warned Lara.
'Don't you dare sink
your teeth into his
trousers!'

'But, Ma!'

'I know,' woofed
Lara. 'I don't like him
either. But the
professor's relying
on us to make a good
impression.'

'I count six,' said Onkers,
looking around the group.

What do you want? thought Star. *A gold star.*

'I was told there'd be eleven of you,'
continued Onkers.

'That's right. Here come the rest,' said
Professor Cortex as Ben, Sophie and Ollie
hurried down the steps, followed by Mr and
Mrs Cook.

'Civilians? You brought civilians?' said Agent Onkers as an excited Ollie ran past him, climbed up into the limo and began jumping on the leather seats.

'Sorry. I'll get him to stop,' said Mr Cook, shoving his sick bag into Onkers' arms and hurrying after Ollie.

Agent Onkers looked horrified.

'I'll deal with that,' said Mrs Cook quietly, taking the sick bag from him and dropping it into a nearby bin. 'And by the way, we're not civilians. We're family.'

Professor Cortex ran a hand through his hair, discovered his bow tie there and hastily pulled it off. 'Agent Onkers, I know how this must look,' he said. 'But we just had a very close shave with the Statue of Liberty and we're not at our best. Wait until you see these Spy Dogs in action. They're amazing.'

'*OK*,' said the American agent,

sounding unconvinced. 'Let's go, shall we?' He swept a hand towards the limo. 'We'll head straight to the FBI field office. Oh, and by the way,' he added, in the most unwelcoming voice he could manage. 'Welcome to New York.'

5. Going Underground

By the time they reached Manhattan, Agent K had recovered enough to let go of Ollie's teddy bear, Spud had slurped up all the crisps and lemonade sticking to his fur, Professor Cortex had borrowed Sophie's hairbrush and Mr Cook was looking much less green.

'That's better, Mum,' said Star, smoothing down the last of Lara's fur. 'We look like we mean business now.'

'So does Agent T,' yapped Spud. 'He hasn't stopped glaring at Agent Onkers!'

'Well, Onkers did call him a baby bunny,' woofed Star.

The limo turned off Fifth Avenue, and pulled up in front of a public square with a fountain.

'Wow! Look at that!' yelled Ollie as they all clambered out of the car. He had spotted a big, glass-fronted toy shop on the far side of the square. 'Is that where we're going?'

The FBI agent slipped on a pair of shades and nodded.

Ollie gave a happy whoop and set off towards the toy shop at a run, but Onkers caught him by the arm and yanked him back. 'Not so fast, kid. We stay together. Understand?'

As Ollie stared up at Agent Onkers, his chin began to tremble. He nodded wordlessly and, when Onkers let him go, Ollie hurried over to Mrs Cook, rubbing his arm.

'Understand?' said Onkers again, this time to the whole group.

Spud gave the FBI agent a glare. *I understand that you're a bully!*

Agent T whipped out his own shades, puffed out his chest and stepped up to the American.

'No, Agent Onkers, I'm not sure we do,' said Professor Cortex as his bodyguard and Agent Onkers eyeballed one another. 'Perhaps you'd like to explain?'

'If you don't stay close to me, you will not gain access to our secret FBI field office,' said Onkers. 'You will be left behind, in the toy shop.'

'We'll look round at the toys later, Ollie,' promised Mr Cook.

'But first, let's go and show Agent Brad Onkers how good we really are, shall we?' said Professor Cortex.

You're on, Prof! Star held her head high as she trotted across the square.

We'll make Onkers eat his words, thought Spud as he trotted alongside Star. *Speaking of eating, when's dinner?*

Inside the toy shop, Onkers led them to the music section. Ben had never seen so many guitars. 'And how cool is that!' he gasped, pointing to a giant piano keyboard set into the floor. Surprisingly, Agent Onkers seemed to be enjoying himself for the first time since they'd met him as he hopped on to one of the keys and it lit up and played a note.

'It's a real piano!' cried Sophie as the agent hopped from key to key.

'I hope he plays chopsticks!' yapped Spud, but the agent stopped and looked their way after only seven notes.

'That wasn't much of a performance,' said Ben.

'It wasn't a performance, kid,' growled

Onkers, pointing at the shelves of saxophones behind them. 'It was an entry code.'

A shelf slid back, revealing an elevator. Quickly, everyone shuffled inside and the shelf slid back into place behind them.

When the elevator door opened again, they stepped out into an underground warren of offices. The FBI emblem was on the wall opposite the lift and, beneath it, a woman in a smart grey skirt and jacket was waiting for them.

Agent Onkers hurried over to her. 'Ma'am, I think we're on to a loser here,' he whispered.

Lara, Spud and Star all bristled.

We heard that, Bonkers!

'Let's wait and see, shall we?' said the grey-suited woman. 'And, Onkers, you'd be wise to remember that dogs have much better hearing than humans.' She winked at Lara, Spud and Star. Turning to the others, she offered a warm smile. 'Welcome, everyone. I'm Amy Whittle, the director of this FBI field office. Professor Cortex, it's wonderful to finally meet you in person. Please follow Special Agent Onkers who will take you and your puppy agents to the test lab. If everyone else would like to come with me, I'll take you to the viewing platform.'

'Good luck, pups!' woofed Lara as they headed off in different directions.

'Don't worry, Mum, we'll make you proud!' yapped Star over her shoulder.

The pups kept their heads high until Lara and the Cooks had disappeared around the corner, but then their tails drooped in unison.

'I'm nervous, bro,' admitted Star.

'Me too,' agreed Spud. 'Do you think we can pass their tests?'

'We'll try our best,' said Star. 'And the prof said he's brought some really good gadgets for us.'

Spud's tail perked up as he eyed the black bag that Professor Cortex was carrying. He loved gadgets. 'I wonder what they are?'

'Let's go and find out,' yapped Star, hurrying after the bag.

A few minutes later, Spud and Star were alone with Professor Cortex in a small room. 'Don't worry, pups,' said Professor Cortex, his eyes sparkling as he unzipped the black bag. 'Whatever tests the FBI have in store for you, these gadgets will help. I designed them with Big City spying in mind – and I think they're my best yet!'

Professor Cortex lifted two black harnesses from the bag. 'This one's for you, Star,' he said, holding up the slightly smaller harness.

Star nodded approvingly as the professor clipped the harness straps into place. *A little black outfit. The classic choice for a girl who wants to impress.*

'Now you, Spud,' said Professor Cortex, slipping the second harness over Spud's head. The harness straps wouldn't quite fasten.

Hmm. Must've been that apple I ate in the limo, thought Spud, conveniently ignoring the three packets of cheese and onion crisps and bottle of lemonade he'd woofed down. He sucked in his tum and snapped the strap buckles shut. *Yup, definitely going to have to cut down on the apples*.

Star pointed to a switch on the harness. *What's this*? she thought, flicking it on and off.

Professor Cortex waved his hands for her to stop. 'That,' he said proudly, 'is a cloaking device.'

And? thought Star. *What does it do?*

'With this you can get through any security gate. You simply hide in a bag and/or suitcase. Flick the switch like so . . . and this little spy pup disappears from scanners and radars.'

And why would I want to be invisible to a scanner? thought Spud. *It's not as if I'm going to be scanned at a supermarket checkout*.

Professor Cortex continued, undaunted by the lack of any enthusiastic tail-wagging. 'So, for example, you can get through airport security,' he said, beaming brightly. 'Benjamin can simply place you in his school bag, switch on your collar and you can pass through the scanner undetected. We can smuggle you to any country in the world. In total secret. Genius, if I say so myself.'

'Very clever,' woofed Star, finally wagging her tail in approval.

'Glad you like it, Star,' beamed Professor Cortex.

'And this one?' yapped Spud, pointing to a small dial.

'Turn it and see,' said the professor. 'I'm sure this one will capture your attention, young Spud.'

Spud twisted the dial and a thin propeller blade sprang from the top strap of the harness. The propeller whirred and he was lifted into the air. 'Whoo-hoo! Is it a bird? Is it a plane? No, it's Superpup!' yapped Spud as he rose up towards the ceiling.

'Just twist the dial up or down to control your height,' said Professor Cortex.

Spud twisted the dial the other way and sank gently back to the floor. The propeller came to a stop and folded back into the top strap of the harness.

'The power cell will only give you two minutes of flight at a time,' warned Professor Cortex. 'But it's enough to get you up to a high window or over a wall. After that, the power cell needs at least ten minutes to charge up again.'

'Amazing, Prof!' woofed Star, wagging her tail even harder. 'I feel ready for anything now!'

'Me too!' yapped Spud, trotting over to the test lab door. 'Come on, sis! Let's show them what we're made of!'

6. Testing Times

Spud eased the door open and the two pups slipped inside. A screen in front of the door stopped them from seeing what was ahead but, when they looked up, they could see that they were in a hall about the same size and height as a sports hall. There was a long window high up in the wall. The Cooks, Lara and Amy Whittle were lined up on the other side of the glass, gazing down at them. The professor had warned them that the FBI would set them a series of tests, both mental and physical. The puppies had done assault courses before, but nothing quite like this.

'What now?' asked Star, looking up at the viewing platform.

Just then Professor Cortex, Agents T and K and Agent Brad Onkers joined the rest of the watchers behind the glass. Amy Whittle gave them a nod. Agent Onkers scowled. Professor Cortex pushed his glasses back up to the bridge of his nose nervously and waved his crossed fingers at the puppies.

'Here we go,' yapped Spud as the screen in front of them slid away.

A voice announced their mission. 'British Spy Dogs – you have various obstacles to overcome. This is the test we give to select our special agents from our standard agents. The world record time is five minutes, fourteen seconds, achieved by our very own Special Agent Bradley Onkers.' Star cast her eyes over the assembled crowd. Onkers curled his lip.

He clearly wants to stay top dog, thought Star. *Let's see if we can knock him off his pedestal.*

'Your time starts as soon as you've chosen your weapon,' boomed the voice.

Spud looked to his left and there was an array of firepower. Hand guns, tasers and automatic rifles. He was tempted by a bazooka. *Too heavy*, he decided, snatching at a water pistol. His sister went for a catapult and three pellets.

A huge digital clock started counting. The lights went out, the red numbers providing the only illumination. The pups' eyes struggled to

focus in the darkness and they nearly jumped out of their fur as an American voice boomed, 'Special agents require special reactions. Eliminate the right people. One wrong shot will end the challenge.'

Suddenly, Star felt her hackles rise. She loaded a pellet into the catapult. There was a scream to the right and a bright light picked out a cardboard cut-out person. Spud and Star almost jumped out of their skins. Spud's paw nearly pulled the trigger and his sister nearly twanged her catapult, but they saw the image was of an old lady.

The pups swivelled, alerted by an evil laugh

behind them. A hooded figure with red eyes loomed at them. Spud resisted firing again, but only just. *Twang!* Star's first pellet hit the hoodie between the eyes and the cardboard person toppled. 'Nice shot, sis,' panted Spud. The pups crept forward, the seconds ticking away. A teacher and a prisoner jumped out at them. Spud squirted his water pistol at the teacher. 'Take that!' he woofed. *Mmm, that felt great!*

His sister floored the escaped prisoner with pellet number two. 'This is good fun!'

The lights came on, and the puppies blinked in the brightness.

Star pointed to a high fence stretching the width of the test lab. 'Next challenge?'

'Easy peasy!' yapped Spud, trotting to the fence and then pressing the hover button on his harness.

'Slow down!' replied Star, running after him. 'We don't know what's on the other side.'

But Spud's paws had already left the ground. 'Time's ticking away, sis,' he woofed, pointing to the clock. 'Not enough time to think and plan.'

Star sighed and pressed her own hover

button. She landed on the top of the fence, saving her valuable battery.

Spud braced his paws against the fence and pushed off into the air. He looked down. 'Nothing, Star,' he woofed. 'It's just a warehouse. I'll land and check it out.' The puppy turned down his hover dial and sank slowly to the ground.

'See, sis? Nothing to worry about,' yapped Spud.

'I'm not so sure,' barked Star, glancing around the dim yard. 'I can smell something . . .'

Spud sniffed. 'You're right,' he yapped uneasily. 'Let's move on. There's a door over there.'

Spud had only taken a couple of steps when a deep, threatening growl came from the darkest corner of the yard.

7. Safe House

Spud gulped. 'H-hello? Who's there?'

Out of the shadows stepped the biggest, meanest-looking dog he had ever seen.

'WHO ARE YOU?!' roared the dog, with drool spraying from its jaws.

'E-excuse me?' yapped Spud. 'Did you spray something?'

'THIS YARD IS MINE. THIS IS MY TERRITORY AND I'M NOT SHARING IT WITH ANYONE.'

'Th-that's absolutely f-fine.' Spud tried to sound calm, but his voice was wobbling. 'It's a lovely yard. You can have the yard. I'll just nip across and be out of your way.' He set off towards the door, but the dog bared its teeth and lunged at him. The puppy dodged the huge animal, but slipped on some slobber and went face first into the floor. *Ouch!*

49

The yard dog was four times the size of Spud. The huge animal turned and growled menacingly, baring its huge teeth.

Spud considered his options. *My black belt karate might be useful, but one swipe of the massive mutt's paw and I'll be knocked sideways. And if I mess with those jaws, it's going to be even worse! And he's guarding the exit so I can either go round him or through him.* The massive dog lunged. *Or over him!* The spy pup hit his hover button and the propeller lifted him into the air.

'COME BACK HERE!' roared the dog, snapping at Spud's dangling paws.

'Ha! Can't catch me now, bonehead!' Spud laughed and wiggled his paws, which made the dog jump even higher. He turned up his hover dial but, instead of rising, he began to fall. *Oops! My power cell's used up!* He looked down at the snapping jaws below. *Goodbye, world!*

His propeller was slowing and his descent quickening. Spud pulled up his paws as he sank towards the dog's sharp teeth. The dog jumped up, but just as it was about to take a bite out of his bum, Star swooshed across the room and caught her brother by his collar.

The beast's jaws crashed shut. The dog shook

his head in anger, but Star and Spud weren't
out of trouble just yet. Spud's extra weight on
Star's propeller meant that they were hanging
at a dangerously low level in the air. The dog
only had to catch up with them to be able to
bite puppy bottoms with one leap.

Star turned up the hover dial to full power
and the pups willed the propeller to move them
faster across to the other side of the room, away
from the rapidly approaching saliva-covered
jaws of the dog. 'We're almost there!' woofed
Spud.

They reached the barrier just as Star's battery ran out. Scrambling over, the puppies collapsed on the floor with a thud.

'Phew! Thanks, Star,' woofed Spud, rubbing his bottom. 'Still, better to have a sore tail than no tail at all!'

Star looked at the clock. 'We've got exactly sixty seconds left. If we want to beat Onkers, that is.'

The puppies looked around at the next part of their challenge. They were in a warehouse set-up, with crates stacked up all around them, but there was one clear pathway stretching all the way from their paws to the exit door at the far end of the test lab.

'Look, Spud,' cried Star. 'We're nearly there! All we have to do is run to the exit. Come on!'

'Wait!' yapped Spud. 'We can't use that pathway!'

Star stopped and frowned at her brother. 'Why not?'

Spud pointed. 'See those thin red lines of light all the way along? They're laser beams. If we cross one of those beams, it'll set off an alarm.'

'So how do we get to the exit?' asked Star.

Spud's tail began to wag. 'Free-running!' he woofed, eyeing the stacks on each side of the pathway. 'Ready, sis?'

'Ready!'

Spud leapt to the right and Star leapt to the left. Together, they raced down each side of the pathway, jumping from crates, bouncing off walls of shelving, rolling down ramps and leaping across gaps. For the last few metres, there was a criss-cross of laser beams that was impossible to navigate. 'This is ridiculous,' panted Spud. 'They've designed it so it's impossible to complete.'

'Nothing's impossible,' replied his sister. 'Remember, this is a test of brains as well as fitness.' Star looked around the huge room. The clock was ticking away. She spied a small box, high up in the corner of the room, a red light blinking. 'That's the power supply to the lasers,' she woofed. Star fumbled for her catapult. She reached for her last pellet. 'A crucial shot,' she said, taking aim and squinting at the blinking light.

Spud watched the digital clock ticking down. *Twelve seconds to go!* he thought as Star released the catapult with a satisfying *twang*. The pups

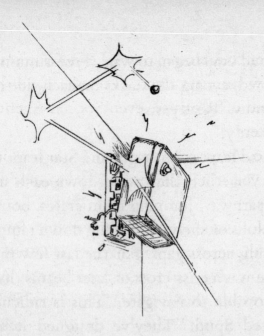

held their breath as the missile bulleted across the room and smashed into the power supply. There was a fizzing sound and some smoke. Then the red light went out and the lasers disappeared.

'Go, go, go,' they heard the professor shout. Star sprinted for the finishing line and hit a big red button. She looked at the clock. It had stopped at five minutes twelve seconds. She high-fived her brother. 'We've beaten Agent Unfriendly by two seconds,' she wagged. 'We are now officially top dogs at the FBI.'

★ ★ ★

When they trotted on to the viewing platform a few minutes later, everyone gave them a round of applause, even Special Agent Brad Onkers.

'So, Agent Onkers,' said Professor Cortex. 'Do you still think they're just a pair of mucky pups?'

'Not at all,' said Onkers, watching Spud and Star thoughtfully with narrowed eyes. 'I admit I completely underestimated them. A very interesting choice of weapons. And shooting a teacher with a water pistol to embarrass instead of hurt, very impressive. I can think of a very good use for those gadgets and those skills.'

'Tell us more about your Spy Dog programme, Professor,' said Amy Whittle.

Professor Cortex went pink with pride. Happily, he began to explain the spy training and the accelerated learning programme the pups had been through. The FBI field director listened with interest, but Brad Onkers never stopped staring at Spud and Star.

'Looks like we've gained a fan,' whispered Star, nudging Spud.

'He's changed his tune,' yapped Spud as Brad gave him a big cheesy grin.

'And Star can speed-read, in several languages,' continued Professor Cortex. 'And I'd put Spud up against your best code-breaker any day. Of course Lara here is their mum. She was an extra-clever dog, even before she started taking my brain formula, and she's passed on her genes to them.'

Lara tried to look modest. *No, really, I'm nothing special. Just because I can do a Rubik's cube in under a minute, beat the prof at chess and sort out Mr Cook's tax return . . .*

'Professor, you and your amazing Spy Dogs have convinced me that this is a project the FBI would like to pursue: with your help, of course,' said Amy Whittle. 'I'm giving you top security clearance.'

'Thanks!' said Professor Cortex, turning an even brighter pink.

'Can you and your men fly to Washington with me tonight? I'd like to introduce you to the head of the FBI.'

'Of course,' spluttered Professor Cortex. 'But what about my Spy Dogs, and the Cooks?'

'Agent Onkers will look after them, won't you, Agent?'

'Don't worry, ma'am,' said Brad. 'I'll take very, very special care of them.'

'This isn't our hotel,' said Mr Cook as the stretch limo pulled up outside a dark house.

'No, sir,' said Agent Onkers from the driving seat. 'This is an FBI safe house.'

'But – we were looking forward to the hotel,' said Mrs Cook, thinking of the lively, friendly-looking place they had booked on the internet.

'This is much more luxurious, ma'am,' said Onkers. 'En suites in every bedroom. I'm sure you're looking forward to a hot bath.'

'But the hotel was next to some good restaurants,' protested Ben, gazing at the quiet street of houses. 'We were going out for pizza.'

Spud's eyes widened and his tail sprang into action.

'I'll have some delivered,' said Onkers, with a hint of annoyance creeping in under his smile.

Bonkers has got an answser for everything, thought Star. *What's he up to?* She looked at Spud, but he was still drooling at the thought of pizza.

'I don't want to stay here,' declared Ollie, folding his arms.

'It's not up to you, son!' snapped the American.

Ollie looked upset. Spud forgot about filling his tum and snuggled up against his favourite member of the Cook family. He glared at Onkers. *Watch it, FBI!*

'You're wrong,' said Sophie stiffly. 'It *is* up to Ollie. He has as much say as anyone in this family.'

'Well said, Soph!' yapped Star, standing up and facing Onkers with her hackles raised.

Brad Onkers looked at the eight rebellious faces in the limo. 'Hey,' he said, raising his hands in a gesture of surrender. 'I'm sorry, guys. I'm only trying to do my job. My boss told me to look after you, and that means keeping you safe. These two pups are really something,' he said, gazing greedily at Spud and Star. 'I have big plans for them tomorrow and I wouldn't want anything to happen to the little guys before then. If you're out wandering the streets of New York, I can't guarantee their safety.'

'Well . . .' Mrs Cook hesitated. 'Maybe just for tonight –'

'Great!' Brad hustled them out of the limo and herded them into the FBI safe house before anyone had a chance to change their mind. Five minutes later, after promising to pick them up first thing in the morning, Agent Onkers had driven away, leaving them in a house filled to the rafters with alarms and panic buttons.

'Bonkers was right; this really *is* a safe house,' woofed Lara, nodding at the bars on the windows. 'They'd keep anything out.'

Star shuddered. 'They're keeping us in too.'

'It's almost like we're prisoners,' agreed Spud, looking at the flashing alarm wired to the front door. 'And why do I get the feeling we're being watched?'

'Pups, I smell a rat,' woofed Lara. 'From now on, I think we need to keep a very special eye on Special Agent Brad Onkers.'

8. Stake-out

Brad Onkers drove away from the safe house, turned a corner and came to a stop. Chad stepped out from the shadows and climbed into the passenger seat.

There were six screens on the limo's dashboard, each showing a different room in the FBI safe house. Five of the screens showed the Cook family as they warily explored their home for the night. The sixth screen showed

Lara, Spud and Star standing with their heads together in the hallway.

'Are you sure they're up to it?' asked Chad, studying Spud and Star. 'They just look like –'

'– a pair of mucky pups,' finished Brad. 'I agree. But you should've seen them today, Chad! They have the skills to steal the Janus mask for us tomorrow night, no problem at all.'

'But how do we –'

'Make them steal it?' Brad gave an evil laugh. 'They'll do anything we ask if it means keeping that black and white mutt and those annoying kids safe.'

'So, if we put the mutt and the kids in danger, then –'

'– the pups will steal the Janus mask to save them,' finished Brad.

The brothers shared an identical evil smile.

'What's the plan?' asked Chad.

'Tomorrow, Chad, you're going to be a second me,' said Brad, pulling an FBI badge from his inside pocket and handing it to his twin. The badge was an exact replica of the one which hung around his neck.

'What's my mission?' asked Chad, rubbing

his hands together as he thought of all the fun he could have, posing as an FBI agent.

'You're taking the mutt, the annoying kids and their parents sightseeing,' said Brad.

Chad pulled a face. 'What? But I hate sightseeing. And I hate kids! Especially that one.' He pointed to one of the screens, which showed Ollie sledging downstairs on a tea tray.

'Count yourself lucky,' said Brad. 'I have to spend the day with those pesky pups!'

'But what am I supposed to do with them?'

'I don't care,' said Brad. 'As long as you make sure they're in the Central Park Zoo after closing time tomorrow tonight.'

'Why the zoo?' asked Chad.

'A zoo can be a very dangerous place.'

Chad's face lit up. 'That's more like it!'

'Here's the plan,' said Brad, leaning closer to his twin.

Brad talked and Chad listened, and the dashboard screens lit up their identical faces like a pair of Hallowe'en masks.

9. The Great Escape

Ollie's eyes were shining as he swung his lightsabre at the head of the stormtrooper. The man ducked and lowered his own lightsabre, which was just what Ollie wanted. He darted in while his enemy's guard was down and drove his lightsabre under the man's breastplate.

'Oof!' said the stormtrooper. He staggered backwards and fell over.

Quick as a flash, Ollie pointed his weapon at the man's throat. 'Victory is mine!' he yelled, planting his foot on the stormtrooper's chest.

'Nice one, kid!' said the stormtrooper, scrambling to his feet and removing his helmet. He winked at Ollie before turning to the crowd that had gathered to watch the fight. 'And our realistic lightsabres are on special offer today, folks! Only twenty dollars each!'

'Did you see that?' cried Ollie, running across to Lara and the Cook family. 'I fought a stormtrooper! This is the best toy shop in the whole world!'

Ollie dashed off to wrestle with a life-sized stuffed gorilla at the front of the store. The Cooks followed, but Lara stayed and watched Brad Onkers take Spud and Star into the secret elevator behind the saxophones. The FBI agent had collected them all from the safe house after breakfast and had outlined the plans for the day while he drove them to the toy shop. Spud and Star were to spend the day training in the underground FBI field office while he, personally, took Lara and the Cooks sightseeing. 'It's the least I can do to make up for my rude behaviour yesterday,' he had said, with an apologetic smile.

Lara frowned. Brad had seemed genuinely sorry, but she was suspicious of his sudden change of heart. She waited until the shelves slid shut again before she turned and trotted after the Cooks.

Spud and Star will be safe inside the FBI field office, she thought. *Whatever Brad Onkers is up to, he can't hurt them if he's spending the day with*

us – and when he comes back, I won't be taking my eyes off him for a second!

From his hiding place behind a Wookie, Chad Onkers watched Lara hurry past. Once she was safely out of sight, he checked his appearance in a nearby mirror. Before they left their house that morning, he and Brad had made sure that they were dressed identically. They had even used the same aftershave. He was confident that he could pass himself off as Brad.

A mutt, some kids and their parents? No problem, he thought, adjusting his FBI badge and stepping out from his hiding place. 'OK, folks,' he said, striding towards Lara and the

Cooks. 'That's the pups settled for the day. Time to go sightseeing!'

The real Brad was still in the underground complex. He had taken Spud and Star to an office and given them a laptop each.

'What do you think we'll be doing, bro?' yapped Star, her eyes shining with excitement as she watched the FBI logo appear on her screen. 'Hacking into criminal organizations? Listening in on top-secret meetings?'

'Maybe we'll be translating coded messages!' woofed Spud as the FBI logo was replaced with a document full of symbols and numbers.

'Wait a minute,' said Star, frowning at her screen. 'Those aren't coded messages. That's a –'

'Maths test,' said Brad. 'I want to assess your intelligence, so you'll both be doing maths tests all day while I take your mum and the Cooks sightseeing.'

Spud and Star stared at Brad in horror.

'All day? No way!' yapped Star.

'If you think we're doing maths tests, you're more bonkers than we thought, Bonkers!' woofed Spud.

'Oh dear,' said Brad, pretending to be

67

concerned. 'You don't look too happy about that. Tell you what, I'll throw in some algebra tests too, just to mix things up a bit.'

Spud jumped down from his chair and marched to the door of the office. 'I'm out of here,' he barked. 'Come on, Star. We're off to find Ma and the Cooks. There's a pastrami-on-rye sandwich out there with my name on it!'

'And I'm booking in for some window-shopping on Fifth Avenue with Sophie,' yapped Star, joining Spud at the door.

'Hold on, pups,' said Brad. 'What's the problem?'

Star jumped back on to her chair and began typing. WE CAME HERE FOR SOME STREET TRAINING AND BIG CITY SPYING!

Brad smiled inside as he read Star's message. This was exactly the reaction he had hoped for! '*We-ell*, I suppose I could take you out on the streets,' he said, with fake reluctance. 'Show you a typical day in an FBI agent's life . . .'

'That's more like it!' yapped Spud, wagging his tail furiously.

'But when we're out there, you have to promise to do exactly what I tell you, however crazy it sounds.'

WE WILL! Star typed.

Brad pretended to be thinking about it. 'OK,' he said finally. 'I'll go and tell the Cooks they'll have to see the sights without me. Listen up; while I'm doing that, you can be completing your first test. The door at the end of this corridor leads to the FBI underground garage. I want you to sneak out of here through the garage, without being detected. I'll meet you outside. If you fail, it's back to the maths tests for you. Agreed?'

Spud and Star both nodded excitedly and raced off along the corridor. Brad smiled as he walked to reception, swiped his FBI card and stepped into the elevator alone. Perfect. Now, as far as his office was concerned, he had left the pups to their maths tests and gone to work. There was nothing to link him to their unauthorized exit from the building.

'Why do you think he wants us to sneak out?' whispered Star as she eased open the door to the underground garage.

'It's our first test,' hissed Spud. 'If we get out

of here unseen, we're in, sis! Proper FBI work! Maybe Onkers isn't so bad, after all.'

Star paused with her paw on the door. 'But remember what Mum said?'

Spud heard Lara's voice in his head. *We need to keep a very special eye on Special Agent Brad Onkers.* He shook the thought away. 'Even Ma can be wrong sometimes.'

Star hesitated, but a day filled with adventure was too good to resist. She opened the door a bit further and they slipped through into the underground garage. It was a grey, concrete space, filled with lines of parked FBI cars. There was a ramp rising from the garage to the street outside. Two armed FBI guards in bulletproof vests stood on each side of a barrier at the bottom of the ramp. They were stopping and checking every car.

'How do we get past the guards?' whispered Star once they had found cover behind a nearby concrete pillar.

'Let me think.' Spud thought so hard, his head began to hurt, but no bright idea came to him. He was about to admit defeat when the door behind them was pushed open. 'Quick! Under that car!' he yapped.

The pups ran to a low, black saloon car and scrambled underneath. Footsteps tapped across the concrete, coming closer and closer. They kept still, waiting for the footsteps to pass them by, but the footsteps stopped right beside them!

There was a beep and the car doors unlocked with a thunk. The driver's door was pulled open and then the chassis sank towards them as someone climbed into the driving seat. Spud looked up to make sure they weren't about to be crushed. He froze, staring at the underside of the car.

'We have to make a run for it!' gasped Star.

'If we're still here when this car drives off, those FBI guards will spot us.'

Spud stayed where he was, staring upwards. 'Star? Remember how we hung from those pipes on that army assault course? The sergeant major said we both had really good muscles.'

'We don't have time for fond memories now!' yapped Star, bracing herself to run when the car engine started.

'Look up,' said Spud. 'See those metal rods? Think you could hang on until the car reaches the top of the ramp?'

Star rolled her shoulders and shook her paws like an athlete at the start of a race. 'I think so,' she yapped.

They each stretched up, grabbed a metal rod in their jaws, wrapped their front paws round it and then swung up their back legs too. The engine started and the whole car began to shake, but they hung on, keeping their tails well out of the way of the exhaust pipe.

The car reversed out of the parking bay and then rumbled towards the barrier. The shaking grew worse, and the exhaust pipe between them was getting very hot. Spud's teeth began to rattle and his jaws ached from holding on so tightly. Star sent him a desperate look as the two guards walked round the car. *I'm not sure I can hang on!*

Hurry up! thought Spud, willing the driver to get a move on.

But the driver was chatting happily with one of the guards while the other guard popped open the boot and checked inside.

Spud felt his back paws slipping. His bum dipped nearer to the concrete.

HURRY UP!

Finally, they heard the whine of the barrier being raised. Star nearly lost her grip as the car bumped over the hump at the bottom of the ramp. She let out a strangled squeak, but managed to scrabble back into position.

Hang on, sis! Nearly there!

The car drove up the ramp and stopped at the top, waiting for a gap in the traffic. Spud and Star dropped from the chassis and lay on their backs under the car, with all their muscles burning. Suddenly, the car roared out into the street, leaving them in the open. They scrambled up and jumped into a hedge, expecting to hear a shout from one of the FBI guards, but nothing happened.

'I think we made it, Spud,' yapped Star after a few minutes. 'The great escape!'

Spud peered out of the bush. He spotted Brad Onkers waiting by a subway sign further down the street. 'There he is,' he yapped. 'I wonder what he has planned?'

'Whatever it is, it has to be better than maths tests,' said Star as they scrambled out of the bush and trotted trustingly towards Brad. 'You never know, bro. We may be in for one of the most exciting days of our lives!'

10. Canine Criminals

'See that guy walking down into the subway?' Brad Onkers muttered from the corner of his mouth. 'Red hair, grey suit, leather briefcase? He's a jewel thief.'

Spud and Star stared at the red-haired man, eyes wide.

'He looks like a baddie,' growled Spud. 'Shifty eyes.'

'You're right, bro,' yapped Star. 'I bet that case is full of diamonds!'

'Let's see how good you pups are at tracking,' said Onkers.

Spud and Star looked at one another, hardly daring to believe what the FBI agent was saying.

'U-us?' yapped Star, pointing at herself and Spud.

'Don't worry. This guy isn't a dangerous

criminal,' said Agent Onkers. 'If he thinks he's being followed, he'll just make a run for it. Your job is not to let him see you. And remember, no need to buy tickets or stop at barriers. I'm making you associate agents for the day. You're with the FBI now!'

Spud and Star hesitated. They didn't know New York at all. How would they find their way back to the FBI field office?

'I'll be right behind you,' said Onkers. '*Your* job is to stay right behind *him*. Now go!'

Spud and Star raced down the steps into the subway station.

'He's gone for the left-hand turnstile!' yapped Star, spotting the red-headed man.

They scrambled on to the ticket office counter, jumped across to the top of the turnstile barrier and then raced down the escalator into the subway.

Agent Onkers smiled as he followed, filming them on his mobile phone. The red-haired man was an innocent traveller, not a jewel thief. The only criminals in that subway station were Spud and Star, and he had footage of them jumping the barrier without paying. What was more, he planned to film them breaking the

law many more times before the day was over.

'Intelligent Spy Dogs? I don't think so.' He sniggered. 'They don't even have the sense to see that I'm setting them up!'

'That was such fun!' gasped Star, twenty minutes later, as they stood in front of Madison Square Garden waiting for Agent Onkers to catch up with them.

'The look on that ticket collector's face when you shot between his legs!' yapped Spud.

'And what about that woman who screamed "rat!" when you ran along the back of the seats in the subway car!' Star laughed.

Spud nodded, but his tail drooped a little.

He felt bad about the woman. Star had been ahead of him. She had not seen how scared the woman was, or how she had spilt her coffee all over her new coat.

Onkers sprinted up the subway steps and hurried across to them. 'Where did he go?'

Spud and Star both pointed at the offices where the red-haired man had finished up. Onkers nodded seriously and wrote down the address in his notebook. 'Good work, agents. Follow me. I'll show you your next mission.'

They hurried after Onkers into Madison Square Garden. An ice hockey game was under way and the roar of the fans echoed through the corridors of the complex. Agent Onkers led them to a door marked STAFF ONLY and they followed him into a space under the stands. A few metres away, beyond a barrier, they could see the New York Rangers on the ice.

Spud and Star crept up to the barrier and watched the game through the criss-cross bars. The teams wore helmets with metal grids on the front. Their skates sliced across the ice like knives and their protective padding made them look like giants. Star winced as two players slammed into the barrier and then tore off again, chasing a brightly coloured disc.

'That disc is called the puck,' Brad explained, shouting to be heard above the roar of the fans. 'Do you think you could steal it for me?'

Spud stared at Brad. *Are you bonkers, Bonkers? One wrong move and we'd be sliced and diced by those blades!*

Star wrote with her paw in the dust. WHY STEAL?

'A gang of criminals are making a lot of money betting on these games,' Brad lied. 'They seem to know which team will win. We think they might have done something to the puck, perhaps put a radio-controlled chip in it. The trouble is, if an FBI agent gets involved, the gang will know we're on to them. But if a couple of pups steal the puck for us . . .'

Star nodded to show she understood. 'What do you think, Spud?' she yapped, watching the teams race after the puck. 'Could we nab it?'

Spud's tail began to wag. 'If it's going to stop a crime, I think we could do it.'

'Let's go then!' yapped Star.

'Geronimo!' woofed Spud as they scrambled over the barrier, jumped on to the ice and skidded towards the puck on their backsides. Behind them, Agent Onkers lifted his mobile phone and started filming. The crowd roared even louder at the sight of two pups joining in the game. Then one of the ice hockey players gave the puck a backwards swipe, and the game changed direction. Suddenly, six beefy men were heading straight for them.

'Yikes!' barked Star, braking with her back paws. 'We'll be squished!'

11. Flying Fish

The puck sailed past them, heading for the barrier. They scrabbled around and ran after it, slipping and sliding. Spud glanced behind him. The hockey players were nearly on top of them! He flung himself on to his belly and sledged across the ice. Star did the same, snatching up the puck with her teeth. The men were close behind. Star didn't dare look, but she could hear their blades cutting into the ice. Just before the pups were about to crash painfully into the barrier, they scrambled to their feet and clawed their way over the top. They landed on the concrete on the other side and without stopping to look back, raced down the players' tunnel to the fire exit beyond.

BLAM!

A second later, half of the New York Rangers team smashed into the barrier behind them.

Spud sat back with a happy sigh, patting his round belly. They were in one of the best restaurants in Manhattan, and he had just slurped up his third plate of pancakes with ice cream and maple syrup.

Star was happy too. They had done everything Agent Onkers had asked of them and, judging by the smile on his face, the FBI agent was impressed with their performance. *I can't wait to tell Mum about our day! Spy Dogs rule! I love working for the FBI.*

Brad Onkers was smiling because he knew that in an hour's time the Janus mask would belong to him and Chad. These pesky spy pups had turned out to be braver, faster and more athletic than he had dared to hope. Even better, he had plenty of footage of them committing crimes all over the city. Once the Janus mask was stolen, he and Chad would get rid of the pups, the Cook family and Lara. He would post his footage on the Internet anonymously. After that, nobody would have any trouble believing that the pups had gone on a crime spree, done away with their family, stolen the mask and made off with it.

He imagined the headlines. *Canine Criminals! Marauding Mutts at the Museum*. His smile broadened. In the face of such a public disaster, the British government would be forced to shut down Professor Cortex's animal spying programme. *I'll make a toast to that,* he thought, downing the last of his beer.

Brad wiped his mouth with the back of his hand and then glanced at his watch. The Metropolitan Museum was about to close. Time to head for Central Park. He reached for his wallet to pay the restaurant bill, but then he had a better idea. 'Don't look now, pups,' he hissed, leaning forward, 'but an old enemy of the FBI has just walked in! I need to get out through the kitchens before he sees me. Can you guys create a distraction? The bigger the better!'

Spud looked at the tables full of food all around him and then he looked at Star. 'Food fight?'

'Food fight,' agreed Star, with a nod.

'Looks like you have a plan,' whispered Agent Onkers, seeing Star nod. 'Why don't you get started? I'll meet you round back afterwards.'

Brad sneaked off towards the kitchens with his head low. Quickly, Spud jumped up on to the table, yapping as loudly as he could to attract attention away from Agent Onkers. Once the whole restaurant was looking at him, he grabbed a pawful of mashed potato and threw it at Star. 'Bullseye!' he barked, splatting Star in the chest.

'You asked for it!' woofed Star, scrambling

on to a table that took her a little closer to the front door. The four diners squealed.

'Shoo, puppy!' one woman cried, flapping a napkin as Star swiped her cream cake.

I'm doing you a favour. A minute on the lips, a lifetime on the hips! Star flung the squishy treat at Spud, catching him full in the face.

'Yum!' slurped Spud, licking cream from his nose.

'Watch out!' yapped Star, pointing over his shoulder.

Spud turned and saw three waiters hurrying towards him with their black coat-tails flapping. *Penguins! It must be feeding time!* He leapfrogged across to a third table, grabbed a whole flounder in his teeth and sent it flying at the waiters like a fishy frisbee. The fish slapped the first waiter in the face and he went over backwards, knocking down the other two as he fell.

Spud was still laughing when a bread roll bounced off his head. Star was now standing on a fourth table, ahead of him. He scooped up a cream cheese bagel and flung it at his sister. Star ducked and the bagel hit the man behind her. The man stood up and threw his half-eaten

burger at Spud. It missed and hit another diner, who threw his pudding across the room.

Soon half the diners were on their feet and food was flying everywhere.

'I think our job here is done, bro,' yapped Star, heading for the door.

Spud followed, shaking cream cake from his ears.

Neither of them noticed Agent Onkers standing quietly at the door to the kitchens, filming the whole thing.

Once they were outside, they raced down the street, ducked into a side alley and then doubled back along the next street. By the time they found Brad waiting by the bins at the back of the restaurant, they had both calmed down and were beginning to feel bad about the chaos they had left behind.

'Did you see that little girl crying because her birthday cake had been squashed?' yapped Star miserably.

Spud's tail drooped. 'Yes. And I've just realized Agent Onkers didn't pay our bill. We ate a lot, sis! Well, I did. And super-sly Bonkers had a steak!'

'Did you see the baddie he was worried about?'

Spud thought back. 'No,' he barked reluctantly. 'I didn't see any new arrivals. Everyone was sitting down eating their meals.'

'OK, pups. Let's go,' said Brad, striding off without giving them a second glance.

'I'm not enjoying this any more,' whimpered Star.

'We have to go with him,' woofed Spud. 'We don't know where we are!' He trotted after Brad. Star was about to follow when she spotted a bright disc sticking out of the top of the bin. *That's the puck we stole from the ice hockey game!*

'Spud!' she hissed. 'Look!'

'Why would Onkers throw it away?' gasped Spud. 'That's supposed to be evidence!'

They looked at one another and then at Brad's retreating back.

'Maybe Mum was right, after all,' yapped Star, saying exactly what Spud was thinking.

'Come on, sis,' he yapped, hurrying after Brad. 'Let's stop being pretend FBI agents and get back to being proper Spy Dogs!'

12. We're All Going to the Zoo

For the hundredth time that day, Lara stared at the man who claimed to be Brad. Ever since he had returned to the toy shop after taking the pups down to the FBI field office, there had been something different about him, something *wrong,* but she couldn't work out what it was.

Same bum-chin. Same horrible aftershave. Same cold-fish eyes. He looks like Brad, he smells like Brad, so why do I think he isn't Brad? Maybe I'm going crazy? She thought back through the day, trying to pin down a reason for her suspicion. She couldn't find one. The FBI agent had been the perfect tourist guide. He had taken them to Central Park, where they had spent hours riding the famous carousel, rowing on the lake, eating huge sandwiches and racing model boats. When Ollie had crashed his model hire boat into a very smart model ocean liner, they had escaped to the Metropolitan Museum of Art. Now they were in a round, windowless room, gazing at the museum's most treasured piece: the priceless Janus mask.

I can't fault him. The Cooks have had a lovely time. They're even calling him Brad now, but I think I prefer 'Not-Quite-Brad'.

'Can we go?' Ollie asked, scuffing the marble floor with his foot.

'In a minute, kid,' said Not-Quite-Brad, gazing at the golden mask.

'But you said we could go to the zoo next! Can we go now? Can we?'

Not-Quite-Brad ignored Ollie and kept on staring at the mask.

'What's up with him?' whispered Sophie.

'I don't know,' Ben whispered back. 'I think he's in *lurve* with that boring old mask!'

Ben, Sophie and Ollie giggled together, and even Mr and Mrs Cook exchanged a smile, but Lara frowned as she watched Not-Quite-Brad. Why was he staring so greedily at the Janus mask? She glanced at the double faces and her eyes widened as an idea began to form at the back of her mind. *Two faces,* she thought, pressing a paw to her brow. *They're the same, but there are two of them . . .*

CLANG-A-LANG-A-LANG!

Lara nearly jumped out of her skin as a bell rang out.

'The museum is closing now,' said the guard. 'Please make your way to the exit, folks.'

'Zoo! Zoo! Zoo! Zoo!' chanted Ollie, leading the way to the main doors.

As Lara brought up the rear, she looked back at the Janus mask, trying to recall the idea that had nearly come to her, but it had gone, chased away by the clanging of the closing bell. Lara shrugged and hurried after Not-Quite-Brad and the Cooks as they made their way through Central Park to the zoo.

'It's closed!' Ollie wailed, pointing at the dark buildings.

'Never mind, Ollie,' said Mr Cook. 'We should be heading back to collect Spud and Star now, anyway.'

'And afterwards we can go to that nice friendly hotel we'll be staying in tonight,' added Mrs Cook, giving Not-Quite-Brad a meaningful look.

Lara nodded her agreement. *Good idea! I'm gasping for a cup of tea and some custard creams!*

'But I wanted to see the polar bears,' said Ollie in a very small voice.

'Tell you what, kid,' said Not-Quite-Brad, walking to a small door in the side of the building. 'As a special treat, I'll take you in to see those bears right now.'

'You can get into the zoo when it's closed?' squeaked Ollie.

'The FBI can get in anywhere!' He blocked the door from view with his body and did something to the lock. When he stepped back again, the door was open.

'Is that – um – legal?' asked Mr Cook.

'Not in my book!' growled Lara, glaring at Not-Quite-Brad.

'Where's Ollie?' asked Sophie.

Lara looked around. Ollie was nowhere to be seen.

'Oh no!' gasped Mrs Cook. 'He must've slipped inside. He's already in the zoo!'

Lara shot through the door after Ollie, imagining him crushed by a python or cornered by a crocodile. She raced down some steps, galloped along a dimly-lit corridor and came out in a large, draughty room with a stainless-steel table and two sinks in the middle. One wall of the room was lined with store cupboards and fridges and freezers full of fruit, vegetables, trays of eggs and boxes of raw meat and fish.

This is where they get the food ready for the animals, she thought. On the other side of the room were huge windows looking out on the polar bear enclosure. Lara sniffed, hoping to find Ollie. Instead she caught the scents of sea lions, penguins and, strongest of all, polar bears! *Ollie wouldn't have gone out there, would he?* she thought, imagining the worst.

'Hello!' Lara whirled around. Ollie was

sticking his head out of the cupboard he had been investigating. 'Isn't this cool!' he cried. 'It's the zoo kitchen.'

Lara slumped with relief. *I thought you were out there trying to be pals with a polar bear!*

'Ollie!' cried Mrs Cook, rushing into the room, followed by the rest of the family. 'How many times have I told you? Don't run off like that!'

'No harm done,' said Not-Quite-Brad. 'Kid, you've come to the right place to see polar bears. If you want, I can get you up close and personal. In fact, I can get you VIP access to the polar bear enclosure!'

'No way!' swooned Ollie.

'Absolutely no way!' hissed Mrs Cook, holding her youngest tightly by the hand.

'Don't worry, Mrs Cook,' purred Not-Quite-Brad. 'It's perfectly safe.' He wandered over to a door at one end of the wall of windows and yanked it open. He threw some fish into the enclosure and locked the door. Everyone moved to the window and watched as two huge bears padded over to the fish and began eating. The fake agent pressed a button and the bears were sealed in a cage.

'See,' smiled Not-Quite-Brad. 'Once the

bears are secure, the zookeeper can get in to their enclosure to clean it and change the water. Come on,' he beckoned, 'let me show you.' He breezed confidently through a second door at the other end of the glass wall and into the bears' enclosure. He stood at the other side of the window and tapped on the glass. 'Come on, guys. The zookeeper does this every single day.'

Delighted, Ollie wriggled out of his mum's grasp with Ben and Sophie running in eagerly behind him. 'Come on then.' Mrs Cook reluctantly beckoned her husband to follow the children with her. Lara stayed close to the family. Something didn't feel right. *And I'm not leaving Bonkers alone until I figure out what it is!*

13. Show Time!

Lara looked around. The polar bears had finished their snack and were pawing at the bars. *My, what big paws you have*, she thought. *And what large teeth!* The small group were standing in a large concrete enclosure. It had steep-sided cliffs of rock which plunged and shelved down to a deep green pool.

'Go and check the temperature of their pool,' suggested Not-Quite-Brad. 'It's f-f-freeeezing!' Ollie, Sophie and Ben didn't need asking twice. Sophie squealed as she dipped her hand into the icy water.

Just then Not-Quite-Brad's phone rang. ''Scuse me, I need to take this,' he said, moving back towards the kitchen door.

Where are you going? Lara padded out of the enclosure after him and caught a glimpse of his phone screen, which showed the name of the person calling. *Brad?* Lara felt a chill run down her spine. *I knew it! But if that's Brad calling, then who are you?*

'Yeah?' said Not-Quite-Brad into his phone. He listened, stepping back into the kitchen. 'Yeah, they're in.'

As Not-Quite-Brad listened to his caller, Lara stared at his face and then at the photograph on the FBI badge around his neck. Finally, she realized what had been bothering her all day. The man in the photograph had a mole on his right cheek, but the man in front of her had a mole on his left cheek.

A twin! Brad Onkers has an identical twin brother! Double agents!

'Yeah, I'll do that right now.' Brad's twin finished his phone call, looked through the window and slammed the door. He turned the key and the lock clicked into place, sealing the family in the polar bear enclosure.

Oh no you don't! Lara leapt at the man. Not-Quite-Brad saw her coming and landed a hefty blow to her mouth. Lara slammed head first into the leg of the table. She lay on the kitchen floor, stunned, waiting for the bells to stop ringing in her head.

'No! Leave her alone!' yelled Ben from behind the glass. Tears dripped down Sophie's face and Ollie clung on to his mum's hand tightly.

'Brad! What are you doing?' asked Mr Cook, knocking furiously on the glass. 'Let us out of here!'

'I'm not Brad. I'm Chad, his good-looking twin,' he shouted, his finger hovering over the cage button.

'You wouldn't,' stammered Mr Cook.

'Oh, I would,' nodded Chad, whipping out his mobile and taking a snap of the terrified family. 'And I will, unless your puppies can save the day.'

★ ★ ★

'Why do you think he's brought us here?' whispered Star.

They were in Central Park, at the back of the Metropolitan Museum of Art. Brad Onkers had moved out of earshot to make a phone call. The museum was closed and there was nobody about. 'I don't know, sis,' Spud admitted. 'But I'm guessing it won't be good.'

'A-are you scared?' whispered Star as they watched Brad stride back towards them.

'Of not-so-special Agent Onkers? Nah,' yapped Spud bravely. 'We could outsmart him any day! We can outrun him too! If all else fails, that's what we do, and then we find our own way back to the toy store. Deal?'

'Deal,' woofed Star, straightening her shoulders.

'OK, pups,' said Brad. 'See that banner on the museum wall?'

Spud and Star looked up. The banner showed a golden mask with two faces. Underneath were the words, 'The Janus mask. More than just a pretty face.'

'The Janus mask is priceless,' Brad explained. 'So the museum has asked the FBI to check their security for them. I've already had a look and I think it's not good enough. I want you to break in and steal the Janus mask to prove it. Of course I'll give it straight back to them afterwards, with some advice on how to beef up their protection.'

'Of course you will!' yapped Spud, backing away from the agent. 'And I'm a monkey's uncle!'

'This is what he's been setting us up to do, bro!' woofed Star. 'He wants us to steal the mask for him. 'Bonkers may be an FBI agent, but he's also a baddie.' She bared her teeth at the man.

'Ah, I see you two have caught on at last,' said Brad. 'Took you long enough. Spy Dogs? I don't think so. Spy Dopes, more like.'

'Shut up, bum-chin!' growled Spud. 'Ready to scarper, sis?'

'On the count of three,' yapped Star. 'One, two –'

'I wouldn't run if I were you,' said Brad, guessing what they were about to do. 'Not before you've had a look at this.' He held up his mobile phone with the screen towards them. It showed the Cooks trapped in an enclosure, with two huge polar bears sticking their noses through the bars of a gate behind the terrified family.

Spud and Star both gasped in horror and Brad sniggered. 'What's the matter, pups? Don't you like this photo? I agree. It's lacking in action. You know what would make it better? If the bears were let out of their cage. What do you think?'

'Don't you dare!' yapped Star.

'Leave our family alone!' snarled Spud.

'Hmm. I'm guessing you want the bears to stay *inside* the cage,' said Brad. 'Trouble is, my twin brother Chad is in Central Park Zoo right now, waiting to open the gate. And unless you steal the Janus mask for me, I'll tell him to go right ahead.' He pressed speed dial and called his brother. 'Put it on video, bro,' he said. Brad turned the screen to face the puppies and they watched as Chad set the timer for ninety minutes. Then Chad's huge face filled the screen.

'I've set the cage to automatically open in ninety minutes,' he beamed. 'So if I were you, little doggies, I'd get that mask. And I'd bring it here pronto.'

Spud and Star looked at each other. 'We have to do it, Spud,' woofed Star. 'If we want to save the Cooks, we have to steal the mask.'

Spud's tail drooped and he nodded.

'Very sensible,' said Brad, pulling their black harnesses from his coat pockets. 'Shall we get started?'

14. Chilled Out

Behind Chad, Lara staggered to her feet. She still wasn't seeing straight, but she had to do something; the Cooks were in danger. *Maybe if I bite Chad's bum hard enough, he'll let them out of there!* Taking a deep breath, she crept forward.

'Don't move another centimetre, you ugly mutt!' said Chad, putting his thumb on the red button which would open the outer gate. 'I've programmed it to open in ninety minutes, but I can just as easily let the bears out now!'

Lara froze instantly, one paw in the air. She knew she had no choice but to do what Chad said.

'That's better,' said Chad, stepping away from the button.

Lara sagged with relief, but the relief didn't last long. When Chad turned to face her, he was holding a gun in his hand. 'Sit!' he ordered.

Lara sat down and tried to look defeated. In fact, she was watching Chad like a hawk, waiting for him to look away so that she could make her next move.

Chad seemed to be reading her mind. He knew she was a Spy Dog so he kept his eyes and his gun trained on her while he walked across to a giant freezer and hauled the door open. 'In,' he ordered, motioning with his gun. 'Or you and your beloved family get it.'

Lara's thoughts were racing. *I don't have any choice! He's got a gun pointing at me and, even worse, a flick of that red button and the kids will be polar bear supper!* Lara walked towards the freezer, exaggerating her limp.

'Nice doggie,' cooed the villain.

Lara took her chance. She launched herself at Chad's gun arm and sank her teeth into his wrist. She growled and tightened her jaws until she could taste blood. The gun went off as Chad staggered backwards. The bullet hit the steel table, ricocheted past Lara's head and embedded itself in the door frame.

Phew! Too close, thought Lara as Chad crashed

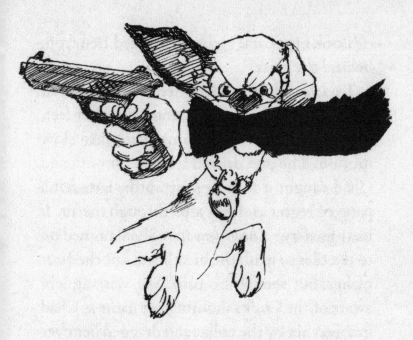

to the ground with her on top of him. *It parted
my hair for me!*

The gun flew from Chad's hand and clattered
under the table. Lara let go of Chad's wrist and
chased the gun, with him scrambling after her.
He grabbed her back leg, but she yanked it
from his grip and put on a burst of speed.
Scrabbling under the table, she snatched the
gun from the floor.

Got it! Now to put it out of harm's reach. She
settled the gun more firmly in her jaws and
burst out from under the table, heading for the
door.

'Look out, Lara!' yelled a muffled Ben from behind the glass.

Too late. Chad cracked her across the head with the metal bowl, knocking her off her feet.

Lara saw stars. Everything went into slow motion. The gun drifted from her mouth and Chad caught it as it flew upwards. Lara felt a pang of regret as she floated through the air. *It was a good try – I nearly made it.* She slammed on to the tiles so hard, the breath was knocked out of her, but she felt no pain. She was vaguely aware of the Cooks shouting her name as Chad grabbed her by the collar and dragged her over to the freezer.

Bags of fish and meat flew past her head as Chad cleared a Lara-sized space inside the cooler. Weakly, she tried to get away from him, but it was no good. Chad picked her up by the scruff of her neck, stuffed her into the freezer and slammed the door. His nostrils flared with fury. He looked at his bleeding wrist and turned the dial to 'maximum chill'.

The pups knew there was no time to lose. They crouched in the shadow of the museum wall, watching two men climb from a plumber's van.

Star glanced over her shoulder, saw the glow of Onkers' mobile phone in the shadows and shuddered. If she and Spud tried to run, Brad would call Chad, and the Cook family would be the main course on a polar bear menu.

'Get ready, sis!' hissed Spud. 'They're coming!'

The men walked across to a door just in front of the pups, put down their toolbags and pressed the intercom button.

'Go!' Spud went for the right-hand bag and Star scrambled inside the other one. They wriggled down inside, trying not to rattle the tools. Both dogs flicked on their cloaking devices.

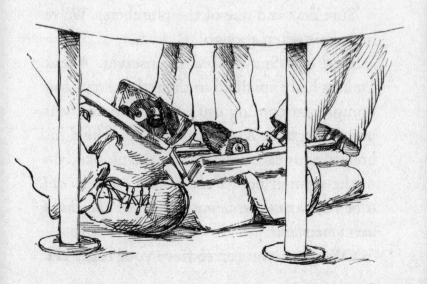

Fingers crossed the prof's invention actually works, thought Star.

'Oooch! Ouch!' breathed Spud as a large spanner poked him in the tum.

'Who is it?' squawked the intercom.

'Plumbing the Depths, here to fix the kitchen dishwasher,' said one of the men.

From their hiding place inside the toolbags, Star and Spud heard a buzz and then a click as the door opened. *Here goes,* thought Star as the bag she was in was picked up. *The start of our criminal career!*

'You know the routine, guys,' said a bored voice, once they were through the door.

'Sure do,' said one of the plumbers. 'We've been here often enough.'

Spud and Star braced themselves. Agent Onkers had explained to them that every bag going in or coming out of the museum was put through an X-ray scanner. Spud held his breath as his bag was lifted up and plonked on to the scanner belt. *If this works, Prof, you can stick as many needles in my bum as you like, and I won't complain!*

'OK, guys, you can retrieve your bags,' the

bored voice said. 'Now, how about a coffee before you start?'

The bags were dropped and then kicked across the floor.

Spud winced as a hammer bashed him on the nose. *Ouch! Watch it! This bag has a soft centre!*

Star heard chairs scraping across the floor. Warily, she prised open the bag and lifted her head enough to peer out. The first thing she saw was Spud's eye, peering back at her. Together, they eased out of the toolbags as quietly as they could. They were under a table, surrounded by three pairs of feet. The door between the kitchen and the dark, empty museum cafe was open.

That's where we need to go, thought Star, remembering the plan of the museum Onkers had shown them on his phone. The puppies waited for their moment. As the feet shuffled towards the kettle, they crept out of the kitchen.

'That was easy, sis!' yapped Spud.

'It was a good start,' Star agreed as they headed into the darkened museum. 'But the most difficult part is yet to come.'

★ ★ ★

The only light was from a small, round window and all Lara could hear was the hum of the freezer. The cold hit her instantly, jolting her wide awake. Her doggie eyes tuned into the darkness and she could see her breath. Lara lay on her side and kicked at the door with all four paws. The door was firmly shut. Lara got to her feet. She stood on her hind legs and peered out of the porthole. She could see the Cooks all waving their arms and shouting at Chad. Chad was sitting at the steel table, ignoring them while he calmly ate an apple.

Lara began to shiver. Quickly, she did a mental check of her injuries. Her head was throbbing and she could feel a lump the size of a plum just behind her sticky-up ear. *At least there's no need for a cold flannel,* she thought, looking at the icy walls around her. *What else?* She could taste blood in her mouth and two of her teeth were hurting. She probed them with her tongue and they wobbled alarmingly. *Hmm, no toffees for a while, and I probably have concussion, but I'll survive. At least, I would do if I wasn't stuck in a freezer.*

Lara had passed a first-aid course as part of her Spy Dog training. She knew exactly what

110

happened when the body temperature dropped too low. She would shiver to start with, as her muscles tried to keep her warm. Then her muscles would give up and she would slowly sink into a sleep too deep to wake up from. *That's if the lack of air doesn't get me first,* she thought, looking at the rubber seal round the freezer door.

Lara's shivering was getting worse. She tried doing a few jumps, but it was no good. She curled up as tight as she could, tucking in her paws and covering her nose with her tail. *I've been in worse situations!* she thought. *I just can't think of one right now. Come on, Spud and Star. It's all down to you now. I only hope you get here in time . . .*

15. Museum Madness

The pups were prowling the corridors of the museum. Star looked at the gift shop on the other side of the corridor. 'I just need to pop in there.'

'This is no time for shopping!' yapped Spud, but Star was already moving.

She had found a bag with 'I ♥ Museums' written on the side. 'Here, hold this,' she woofed, handing it to Spud. 'We'll need something to carry the mask in.'

'Good thinking,' said Spud, glancing over his shoulder at a spooky-looking mummy whose shrivelled bandaged face seemed to follow their every move. 'Shall we go?'

But Star was flicking through an exhibition catalogue. 'It says here the Janus mask weighs half a kilo. We need to find something that weighs exactly the same.'

Spud headed straight for the sweets. 'Let's see,' he muttered, filling a paper bag with an assortment of sweets. 'Cola cubes, toffees, mints – my mouth's watering! Ah, there we are,' he woofed, looking at the scales. 'Exactly half a kilo.' Star folded the bag into a neat parcel and slipped it under her harness straps.

'There,' she giggled. 'Now I look as round as you!'

'I'm not round!' protested Spud. 'I'm well built.'

'Shhh!' Star pointed to the gift shop doorway.

Spud listened and heard dragging footsteps in the corridor outside.

The mummy! The mummy's coming to get us!

They ducked behind a bin of dinosaur toys. Spud closed his eyes as the dragging footsteps drew nearer, reached the door and stopped.

'Oh, m-mummy!' he quavered, opening one eye.

A cleaner was bent over in the doorway, picking up a piece of paper. The man straightened up and carried on down the corridor, pushing a broom in front of him.

Spud heaved a sigh of relief. Together, they crossed the corridor behind the cleaner and scurried over to the tunnel that would take them into the Janus mask room.

'There's our first challenge,' woofed Spud, nodding at the slanting red beams criss-crossing the tunnel. 'Laser beams. Only this time we can't go round the edge like we did in the FBI test lab.'

Star studied the beams. 'They're meant to detect a human, though, not little pups like us. They might just be far enough apart for us to squeeze through. Ready?'

'We don't have a choice, sis.'

Star went first, and Spud followed in her paw prints. They slid under the first beam without any problem, but then they had to rise up on to their back paws and edge sideways until they could dive over the second beam. A forward roll took them under the third, but the next few beams were criss-crossed together in a tangle of red light.

'We can do it,' breathed Star. 'It'll be just like playing Twister, and we beat everyone last Christmas, remember?'

They stepped, tumbled and scissor-jumped their way across, sometimes with less than a centimetre to spare. The only way to beat the very last beam was to edge under it like limbo dancers. Star went first, but when Spud tried to follow, he ran into problems.

'Watch your tum!' hissed Star.

Spud sucked in his breath and shuffled under.

'Watch your nose!'

Spud groaned, bent backwards another few centimetres and then collapsed on to his back. Star grabbed his hind legs and dragged him out of the tunnel like a sack of potatoes.

'No problem,' panted Spud, jumping up with a flourish and surveying the room. A security camera winked from the ceiling, but they weren't worried about that. Agent Onkers had sent a signal from his phone to the museum cameras, putting them on a loop which repeated the same five minutes of footage. Anyone watching from the security office would think the Janus mask room was empty.

The mask gleamed on its pedestal, but Spud

and Star were more interested in the circle of floor around it.

'There's the top of the cylinder,' yapped Star, pointing to the steel circle in the floor around the pedestal. 'If anything hits the floor on the other side of this barrier rope, the cylinder shoots up and seals the Janus mask inside.'

'So we don't let *anything* drop!' woofed Spud, helping his sister to pull the museum bag out of her harness straps. They took one handle each and then switched on their hovers. The propeller blades opened out and they were lifted into the air. 'Remember, they have a very short battery life,' said Star.

They stuck their hind legs out and pushed off from the wall so that they drifted out into the middle of the circle.

'Here we go,' said Spud, looking down at the Janus mask. Carefully, they let themselves sink down until they were centimetres above the mask. Spud lifted the bag of sweets and Star got ready to grab the mask.

'Remember, it has to be seamless,' said Star. 'The instant I lift the mask, you have to drop the sweetie bag.'

Spud nodded. The smell of the sweets under

his nose was starting to make his mouth water. A drop of drool appeared at the corner of his mouth.

'The pressure pad under the mask is very sensitive,' Star continued. 'If it senses the slightest change, it will trigger an alarm.'

Spud waved his paws frantically. *Get on with it!* The drop of drool was getting bigger by the second. Soon it would fall from his jaws and on to the floor, and then the cylinder would shoot up through the floor, trapping them inside!

'OK, here goes.' Star wiggled her bum and took a deep breath. Spud sucked hard, trying to keep the drool in place just a little longer.

Star grabbed the mask, Spud let go of the sweets, the pressure pad alarm stayed silent, but the drop of drool fell from his mouth. In slow motion, he watched it tumble towards the floor.

'Nooooo!' Desperately, he swished his tail and whacked the drop of drool. The puppies watched as it landed just outside the security ring. *Phew!* Spud nearly fainted with relief.

Star eased the mask into the bag and they began to do doggy-paddle in the air. At first,

nothing happened, but then they began to move jerkily through the air back to the barrier rope. As they went, they sank nearer and nearer to the floor as their hover power cells ran down.

'Close one!' gasped Star as they scraped over the rope and landed in a heap. 'In fact, far too close for comfort!'

Wrapped up in the bag, the Janus mask fitted

snugly against Star's chest under the harness straps. 'Much flatter,' she yapped, patting her tummy. They set off, weaving and dancing through the lasers for a second time. Diving over the last beam, they rolled out into the corridor. 'We made it!' whispered Star.

'Not quite,' replied Spud, pointing to the clock on the wall. 'We only have a few minutes before they take out the rubbish!'

They raced down the stairs to a small room stacked high with black rubbish bags. They heard footsteps. 'Quick! Someone's coming!' panted Star, pulling open the top bag.

'Pooey!' choked Spud. 'Mouldy cheese and rotten tomatoes!'

'No choice,' hissed Star, taking a deep breath and diving in. Spud groaned but followed Star into the stinking mess. His paws sank into something squishy and a worm of cold spaghetti slid down his back. Star grabbed him and they clung together with the Janus mask sandwiched between them.

A second later, the top of the bag was pulled open. Spud felt his heart stop. It was all over – they were about to be discovered. *We were so close! What'll happen to Ma and the Cooks now?*

'Phwoar!' They heard the cleaner cough. 'That stinks worse than this does!'

Spud and Star slapped their paws over their noses as the cleaner dumped a carton of disgustingly sour milkshake over their heads and tied the bag shut. The pups clung together, hardly daring to believe their luck as the cleaner flung their smelly bag out through the basement door. They were out!

16. The Gold Trail

'You really stink!' said Brad Onkers for the third time in as many minutes.

'Yeah, well, at least we can wash the smell off,' muttered Spud. 'You're stuck with being ugly for life!'

They followed Brad through the zoo grounds. Chad had left the gate unlocked for them. They passed barking sea lions at the entrance, and then a pool with plexiglass walls, where penguins swam past them at eye level.

'Get a move on,' Onkers ordered, bounding up some steps. 'I can't wait for Chad to see this!' He held up the bag with the mask inside.

'And I can't wait for you both to see the inside of a prison,' yapped Star as she and Spud trotted up the steps after the FBI agent. To their right was another window, showing a deep, empty pool. 'I wonder what that belongs to?' she wondered.

'Them,' yapped Spud as they reached a viewing platform at the top of the steps. The pool shone green below them and, over at the other side of the enclosure, two huge polar bears crouched in a small cage. Ollie, Ben and Sophie were huddled together on the concrete platform beside the cage, watching Mr and Mrs Cook pound their fists against the wall of reinforced glass behind them.

'At least Chad hasn't opened the cage yet,' breathed Star. 'Come on. Time for Bonkers to keep his side of the bargain.'

When they reached the zoo kitchen, the pups saw Chad munching an apple while Mr and Mrs Cook still hurled their fists at the glass. Mrs Cook wailed even louder when she saw Star and Spud. 'Help!' came her muffled screech from behind the glass. 'We're in here. And poor Lara's in there,' she said, pointing to the freezer.

Spud ran to the freezer and scraped at the door. He leapt up at the handle, but it was far out of his reach. 'Let her out now, Bonkers!' he barked at Brad.

The two brothers laughed their identical laughs.

Chad looked at his brother. 'I think these stupid mutts actually . . .'

'. . . believed us,' chuckled Brad. 'They thought we would let everyone go home! I love . . .'

'. . . happy endings,' laughed Chad. The brothers looked each other in the eye and their smiles were gone. 'And there's nothing happier than everyone dying together,' remarked Chad.

'But – you promised,' whimpered Star.

'Time to die,' snarled Brad.

Chad pulled a gun from his jacket. Brad put the bag with the Janus mask on the table and moved towards them at a crouch with his arms spread. 'Come here, mutts!'

Spud and Star had nothing to lose. They moved as a team, jumping up on to the table and grabbing the museum bag between them. They skidded across the steel surface, falling to the floor below. The breath knocked out of them from the impact, Star and Spud raced as hard as they could out of the kitchen dragging the bag, with Brad and Chad only a few steps behind.

Spud and Star panted with the effort of carrying the mask's weight, knowing the brothers would catch them long before they reached the main gate. They heard a shot. *Missed!* A bullet embedded itself into the wall beside them and they sprinted faster than ever. Desperately, they swerved on to the viewing platform above the polar bear pool, and scrambled up on to the top of the wall. The puppies looked at each other.

'You ready?' woofed Spud.

'Let's go!' barked his sister and the brave puppies launched themselves into the pool with a terrified yowl.

Spud spluttered to the surface, closely followed by his sister. 'Boy, this is cold,' she whined, paddling furiously to the side. The twins appeared on the viewing platform.

'Come back here with our mask,' yelled a purple-faced Chad.

Spud heaved himself out of the icy water and shook himself, water spraying everywhere. He

jabbed a paw to the centre of the pool. Chad went a darker shade of purple as he saw the priceless Janus mask slowly sink to the very bottom of the murky pool.

Greed glinting in their eyes, the baddies leapt into the air and plunged into the polar bears' pool.

17. The Bear Necessities

Coughing and wheezing, Brad and Chad surfaced and floundered across the deep pool. The priceless Janus mask was glinting below. Chad doggy-paddled ahead of Brad and hauled himself out. He took his gun and pointed it at Star.

Noooo! Spud woofed.

Star froze.

Chad pulled the trigger and there was a watery *phut*, but no bullet. He screamed in frustration and emptied the water from his gun. He shot again, with the same result.

'Forget the blasted dogs!' yelled Brad from the pool. 'It's the mask we're after,' he said, taking a huge breath and plunging underwater.

Everyone watched as the man in the suit dived down to the bottom of the pool before surfacing, empty-handed and empty-lunged. 'You get it, idiot,' he bellowed to his brother. Chad dived back into the water. A minute later, he surfaced, Janus mask in hand. He struggled to the water's edge, a victorious grin on his face, as his brother hauled him out.

'Yes! We got it!' Brad punched the air. But the brothers' joy was short-lived as they watched the puppies twist the dial on their harnesses and hover up to the viewing platform, leaving the twins trapped.

'Bye bye, boys!' yapped Spud. 'Don't worry about missing us — you'll have company soon enough!'

Seconds later, the puppies were back in the zoo kitchen. Spud crouched as Star climbed on to his shoulders. She used her mouth and paws to turn the key and the Cook family burst in through the door.

'Thank goodness,' yelled Mrs Cook as the door was bolted behind her. 'Just in time. Those bears were getting hungry!'

A bell rang as the ninety minutes were up. The family looked through the window and watched as the cage bars disappeared. The polar bears sniffed the air and padded down towards the pool to see what food the keeper had left for them. Whatever it was smelt tastier than their usual bucket of fish. Ben winced.

'Forget the baddies for a minute,' barked Star. 'Quick! Get Mum!' But Sophie was already on her way. She grabbed the freezer door handle and yanked it open. Cold air billowed out.

'Is she still alive?' yapped Spud as Mr Cook reached in, scooped Lara out and carried her over to the table. Spud and Star jumped up beside her and nuzzled her fur. Lara was as cold as ice.

'Ma!' whimpered Spud. 'We're sorry! This is all our fault. We should have listened to your warning.'

'We thought it was exciting, going off with Brad instead of staying in the field office,' sobbed Star. 'We thought we were being proper Spy Dogs, but we were just being silly pups.'

'What'll we do, without you to keep us on

the right track?' whispered Spud, licking Lara's cold face.

Star cried into Lara's sticky-up ear.

The Cooks were all crying too. Ben rested his hand on his beloved pet's chest.

'I can't believe she's gone,' sobbed Sophie.

'She isn't,' said Ben, looking down at his hand. It was rising and falling in time with Lara's shallow breaths. 'She's still alive!'

'We need to warm her up!' cried Mrs Cook, pulling off her jacket.

Mr Cook yanked his jumper over his head and the Cook children added their coats to the pile on the table.

'Lift her on to the coats,' instructed Mrs Cook. 'Good. Now cuddle her, everybody. Give her our warmth.'

Spud and Star both squeezed in between Lara's front legs, Ben clambered on to the table and cuddled her back, Sophie and Ollie took a back paw each and held it between their hands, while Mr and Mrs Cook bent over the table and wrapped their arms round her in a massive team hug.

When Lara opened her eyes, she saw her pups and then the faces of the Cook family. She felt their arms encircling her. Her head ached fiercely and her paws burned with pain as the feeling returned, but she had never felt so safe and happy.

A few minutes later, she felt strong enough to stagger to her feet. 'Where are they?' she croaked.

'The terrible twins? Follow me, Ma,' yapped Spud.

He and Star led the way out to the polar bear viewing platform. Mr Cook followed, carrying Lara in his arms.

'That looks uncomfortable,' chuckled Sophie, gazing down at Brad and Chad. They were clinging together on the point of a narrow needle of rock, clutching the Janus mask between them. The polar bears paced below.

'I'm not sure I like polar bears any more,' said Ollie.

'Oh, they're only being bears, Ollie,' said Mr Cook. 'The real baddies are the ones holding the mask.'

'Their balance is *very* good,' yapped Star, watching the brothers wobble on their perch.

'Yes, they seem to be "bearing up" well,' joked Lara feebly.

Mrs Cook dialled 911. 'Hello? We need a doctor, right away. Or maybe a vet? Also, if you'd like to send the police to Central Park Zoo, they can nab two baddies for the price of one!'

'I'd like to leave them there all night after

what they did to Lara,' growled Ben as the sirens wailed towards them across Central Park. 'But I suppose I'll just have to grin and "bear" it.'

18. New York, New York!

Mrs Cook wasn't looking too pleased. Professor Cortex was showing them Agent Onkers' secret video footage on his laptop. The Cooks had held their breath as Star and Spud risked their lives to steal an ice hockey puck. Mrs Cook glared as the food fight started.

'We thought it was a mission,' wagged Star, her guilty eyes looking up at the family. 'We were being tricked.'

'Yeah,' agreed her brother. 'Why else would I be throwing food instead of eating it?'

Professor Cortex tried to smooth things over. 'It seems that the puppies put an end to a very dangerous escapade,' he began. 'Not only were you lot all to be fed to the bears, but the pups were then going to be framed for it.' The scientist mopped his brow. 'Very dangerous

133

indeed. The Onkers twins had accounted for nearly everything.'

Except super special secret agents Star and Spud, thought Star, puffing out her chest with pride.

'The FBI is very grateful,' said Professor Cortex, beaming round the table. They were gathered in the big dining room at the hotel, and the table was groaning under the weight of every kind of New York delicacy, from pizzas to donuts. 'This is their way of saying thank you.'

Spud tried to say, 'They're very welcome,' but all he could manage through a mouthful of pastrami was '*Mpphh!*'

'When they broke into the Onkerses' house, they found it stuffed full of stolen artworks,' continued the professor.

'Bonkers and Conkers have certainly been busy!' yapped Star.

'I knew that Brad was a bad un from the start,' said Agent T smugly. Agent K nodded in agreement and they clinked their cups together.

'Now that they're behind bars, all I want to do is enjoy the rest of our holiday,' said Mr Cook.

'That reminds me,' said the professor, pulling a wad of tickets from his jacket. 'The FBI would also like you to have these. Family tickets to all the major attractions in New York, including Broadway shows, access to the Empire State Building and the Yankee Stadium, tea at the Waldorf Hotel, tickets for the Coney Island funfair and vouchers for all the big Fifth Avenue stores.'

Ben and Sophie cheered, and Ollie leapt out of his seat and ran three times round the room.

'Humph. That's the least they can do, after we nearly got eaten and poor Lara nearly froze,' said Mrs Cook.

Lara pulled her shawl tighter round her shoulders, remembering the bone-numbing cold inside the freezer. Star and Spud cuddled up protectively to their mum.

'Finally, before we get stuck into all this

lovely food, I'd just like to say that I'm very proud of my three Spy Dogs,' said the professor, smiling at Lara, Spud and Star. 'Once again, they put their lives on the line against a very nasty pair of baddies. And I think we'd all agree that Spud and Star have passed their Big City spy training with top marks. Give me a spy pup over the FBI any time!'

'Hear, hear!' said Mr and Mrs Cook as Ben, Sophie and Ollie all clapped in agreement.

'And,' added the professor mischievously, 'raise your glasses to the spy pups' next mission . . . at the North Pole!'

Spud nearly choked on his donut. Star slammed his back as he coughed it back up. *No more polar bears!*